Rudyard Kipling was born in
remained for the first fi
experiences, and his subseq
England, inform much of hi
be seen throughout his wor
where he worked as a journal.
short stories and poems, and
favour with the critics of the
Dickens, he went on to write some of his most famous novels,
notably the Jungle Books and *Captains Courageous*. When
tragedy struck his family with the death of his daughter in 1899
followed by the death of his only son in 1915, his work
inevitably took on a darker, more sombre tone and he remained
preoccupied with the themes of psychological strain and
breakdown until his death in 1936.

Kipling's reputation varied enormously both within his
lifetime and in subsequent years. At one time hailed a genius
– indeed Henry James called him 'the most complete man of
genius I have ever known' – and awarded the Nobel Prize for
Literature, he later became increasingly unpopular with his
paternalistic and colonial views being seen as unfashionable in
the extreme. However the enduring appeal of works such as
Kim, the *Just So Stories*, and the Jungle Books has done much
to redress the balance in recent years and he is once again
regarded as the outstanding author that he is.

BY THE SAME AUTHOR
ALL PUBLISHED BY HOUSE OF STRATUS

UNDER THE DEODARS

BY RUDYARD KIPLING

This edition published in 2002 by House of Stratus, an imprint of
Stratus Books Ltd., 21 Beeching Park, Kelly Bray,
Cornwall, PL17 8QS, UK.

www.houseofstratus.com

Typeset, printed and bound by House of Stratus.

A catalogue record for this book is available from the British Library
and the Library of Congress.

ISBN 1-84232-960-X

The Publisher would like to thank The Kipling Society for all the support they
have given House of Stratus Ltd. Any enquiries about the Society please contact:
The Kipling Society, The Honorary Secretary, 6 Clifton Road, London, W9 1SS.
Website: www.kipling.org.uk

"And since he cannot spend nor use aright
   The little time here given him in trust,
But wasteth it in weary undelight
   Of foolish toil and trouble, strife and lust,
He naturally clamours to inherit
The Everlasting Future that his merit
   May have full scope – as surely is most just."

– *The City of Dreadful Night.*

PREFACE

Strictly speaking there should be no preface to this, because it deals with things that are not pretty and uglinesses that hurt. But it may be as well to try to assure the ill-informed that India is not entirely inhabited by men and women playing tennis with the Seventh Commandment; while it is a fact that very many of the lads in the land can be trusted to bear themselves as bravely, on occasion, as did my friend, the late Robert Hanna Wick. The drawback of collecting dirt in one corner is that it gives a false notion of the filth of the room. Folk who understand and have knowledge of their own, will be able to strike fair averages. The opinions of people who do not understand are somewhat less valuable.

In regard to the idea of the book, I have no hope that the stories will be of the least service to any one. They are meant to be read in railway trains and are arranged and adorned for that end. They ought to explain that there is no particular profit in going wrong at any time, under any circumstances or for any consideration. But that is a large text to handle at popular prices; and if I have made the first rewards of folly seem too inviting, my inability and not my intention is to blame.

RUDYARD KIPLING

CONTENTS

THE EDUCATION OF OTIS YEERE

Part I

SHOWING HOW THE GREAT IDEA WAS BORN.

> "In the pleasant orchard-closes
> 'God bless all our gains,' say we;
> But 'May God bless all our losses,'
> Better suits with our degree."
> — *The Lost Bower.*

This is the history of a Failure; but the woman who failed said that it might be an instructive tale to put into print for the benefit of the younger generation. The younger generation does not want instruction. It is perfectly willing to instruct if any one will listen to it. None the less, here begins the story, where every right-minded story should begin; that is to say at Simla, where all things begin and many come to an evil end.

The mistake was due to a very clever woman making a blunder and not retrieving it. Men are licensed to stumble, but a clever woman's mistake is outside the regular course of Nature and Providence: since people know that a woman is the only infallible thing in this world, except Government Paper of the '79 issue, bearing interest at $4^1/_2$ per cent. Yet we have to remember that six consecutive days of rehearsing the star part of *The Fallen Angel,* at the New Gaiety Theatre where the

1

plaster was not properly dry, might have brought about an unhingement of spirits which, again, might have led to eccentricities.

Mrs Hauksbee came to "The Foundry" to tiffin with Mrs Mallowe, her one bosom friend; for she was in no sense a woman's woman. And it was a woman's tiffin, the door shut to all the world; and they both talked mysteries.

"I've enjoyed an interval of sanity," Mrs Hauksbee announced, after tiffin was over and the two were comfortably settled in the little writing room that opened out of Mrs Mallowe's bedroom.

"My dear girl, what has he done?" said Mrs Mallowe sweetly. It is noticeable that ladies of a certain age call each other "dear girl," just as Commissioners of twenty-eight years' standing address their equals in the Civil List as "my boy".

"There's no he in the case. Who am I that an imaginary man should be always credited to me? Am I an Apache?"

"No, dear, but somebody's scalp is generally drying at your wigwam door. Soaking rather."

This was an allusion to the Hawley Boy who was in the habit of riding all across Simla in the Rains, to call on Mrs Hauksbee. That lady laughed.

"For my sins, the Aide at Tyrconnel last night told me off to The Mussuck. Hsh! Don't laugh. One of my most devoted admirers. When the duff came in — someone really ought to teach them to make puddings at Tyrconnel — The Mussuck was at liberty to attend to me."

"Sweet soul! I know his appetite," said Mrs Mallowe. "Did he, oh, did he begin his wooing?"

"By a special mercy of Providence, no. He explained his importance as a Pillar of the Empire. I didn't laugh."

"Lucy, I don't believe you."

"Ask Captain Sangar; he was on the other side. Well, as I was saying, The Mussuck dilated."

"I think I can see him doing it," said Mrs Mallowe, pensively, scratching her fox terrier's ears.

"I was properly impressed. Most properly. I yawned openly. 'Strict supervision, and play them off one against the other,' said The Mussuck, shovelling down his ice by tureenfuls, I assure you! '*That*, Mrs Hauksbee, is the secret of our Government.'"

Mrs Mallowe laughed long and merrily. "And what did you say?"

"Did you ever know me at a loss for an answer yet? I said: 'So I have observed in my dealings with you.' The Mussuck swelled with pride. He is coming to call on me tomorrow. The Hawley Boy is coming too."

"'Strict supervision and play them off one against the other. *That*, Mrs Hauksbee, is the secret of *our* Government.' And I daresay if we could get to The Mussuck's heart we should find that he considers himself a man of the world."

"As he is of the other two things. I like The Mussuck, and I won't have you call him names. He amuses me."

"He has reformed you too, by what appears. Explain the interval of sanity, and hit *Tim* on the nose with the paper-cutter, please. That dog is too fond of sugar. Do you take milk in yours?"

"No, thanks. Polly, I'm wearied of this life. It's hollow."

"Turn religious, then. I always said that Rome would be your fate."

"Only exchanging half-a-dozen *attachés* in red for one in black, and if I fasted the wrinkles would come and never, never go. Has it ever struck you, dear, that I'm getting old?"

"Thanks for your courtesy. I'll return it. Ye-es, we are both not exactly – how shall I put it?"

"What we have been. I feel it in my bones. Polly, I've wasted my life."

"As how?"

"Never mind how. I feel it. I want to be a Power before I die."

"Be a Power, then. You've wits enough for anything – and beauty."

Mrs Hauksbee pointed a teaspoon straight at her hostess: "Polly, if you heap compliments on me like this I shall cease to believe that you're a woman. Tell me how I am to be a Power."

"Inform The Mussuck that he is the most fascinating and slimmest man in Asia, and he'll tell you anything and everything you please."

"Bother The Mussuck! I mean an intellectual Power – not a gas power. Polly, I'm going to start a *salon*."

Mrs Mallowe turned lazily on the sofa, and rested her head on her hand. "Hear the words of the Preacher, the son of Baruch," she began.

"Will you talk sensibly?"

"I will, dear, for I see that you are going to make a mistake."

"I never made a mistake in my life – at least, never one that I couldn't explain away afterwards."

"Going to make a mistake," went on Mrs Mallowe, composedly. "It is impossible to start a *salon* in Simla. A bar would be much more to the point."

"Perhaps, but why? It seems so easy."

"Just what makes it so difficult. How many clever women are there in Simla?"

"Myself and yourself," said Mrs Hauksbee, without a moment's hesitation.

"Modest woman! Mrs Feardon would thank you for that. And how many clever men?"

"Oh – er – hundreds," said Mrs Hauksbee vaguely.

"What a fatal blunder! Not one. They are all bespoke by the Government. Take my husband, for instance. Jack used to be a clever man, though I say so who shouldn't. Government has eaten him up. All his ideas and powers of conversation – he really used to be a good talker, even to his wife, in the old days – are taken from him by this – this kitchen sink of a Government. That's the case with every man up here who is at work. I don't suppose a Russian convict under the knout is able to amuse the rest of his gang; and all our menfolk here are gilded convicts."

"But there are scores – "

"I know what you're going to say. Scores of idle men up on leave. I admit it, but they are all of two objectionable sets. The Civilian who'd be delightful if he had the military man's knowledge of the world and style, and the military man who'd be adorable if he had the Civilian's culture."

"Detestable word! Have Civilians culchaw? I never studied the breed deeply."

"Don't make fun of Jack's Service. Yes. They're like the teapoys in the Lakka Bazar – good material but not polished. They can't help themselves, poor dears. A Civilian only begins to be tolerable after he has knocked about the world for fifteen years."

"And a military man?"

"When he has had the same amount of service. The young of both species are horrible. You would have scores of them in your *salon*."

"I would not!" said Mrs Hauksbee fiercely. "I would tell the bearer to turn them out. I'd put their own Colonels and Commissioners at the door to turn them away. I'd give them to the Topsham Girl to play with."

"The Topsham Girl would be grateful for the gift. But to go back to the *salon*. Allowing that you had gathered all your men and women together, what would you do with them? Make them talk. They would all with one accord begin to flirt. Your *salon* would become a glorified 'Scandal Point' by lamplight."

"There's a certain amount of wisdom in that view."

"There's all the wisdom in the world in it. Surely, twelve Simla seasons ought to have taught you that you can't focus anything in India; and a *salon*, to be any good at all, must be permanent. In two seasons, your roomful would be scattered all over Asia. We are only little bits of dirt on the hillsides – here one day and blown down the road the next. We have lost the art of talking – at least our men have. We have no cohesion – "

"George Eliot in the flesh," interpolated Mrs Hauksbee wickedly.

"And collectively, my dear scoffer, we, men and women alike, have no influence. Come into the verandah and look at the Mall!"

The two looked down on the now rapidly filling road, for all Simla was abroad to steal a stroll between a shower and a fog.

"How do you propose to fix that river? Look! There's The Mussuck – head of goodness knows what. He is a power in the land, though he does eat like a costermonger. There's Colonel Blone, and General Grucher, and Sir Dugald Delane, and Sir Henry Haughton, and Mr Jellalatty. All Heads of Departments, and all powerful."

"And all my fervent admirers," said Mrs Hauksbee piously. "Sir Henry Haughton raves about me. But go on."

"One by one, these men are worth something. Collectively, they're just a mob of Anglo-Indians. Who cares for what Anglo-Indians say? Your *salon* won't weld the Departments together and make you mistress of India, dear. And these creatures won't talk administrative 'shop' in a crowd – your *salon* – because they are so afraid of the men in the lower ranks overhearing it. They have forgotten what of Literature and Art they ever knew and the women – "

"Can't talk about anything except the last Gymkhana, or the sins of their last wet nurse. I was calling on Mrs Derwills this morning."

"You admit that? They can talk to the subalterns though, and the subalterns can talk to them. Your *salon* would suit their views admirably, if you respected the religious prejudices of the country and provided plenty of places to flirt in."

"Oh, my poor little idea! Shaded nooks in a *salon!* But who made you so awfully clever?"

"Perhaps I've tried myself; or perhaps I know a woman who has. I have preached and expounded the whole matter and the conclusion thereof – "

"You needn't go on. 'Is Vanity.' Polly, I thank you. These vermin" – Mrs Hauksbee waved her hand from the verandah to two men in the crowd below who had raised their hats to her – "these vermin shall not rejoice in a new 'Scandal Point' or an extra Peliti's. I will abandon the notion of a *salon*. It seemed so tempting, though. But what shall I do? I must do something."

"Why? Are not Abana and Pharphar – ?"

"Jack has made you nearly as bad as himself! I want to, of course. I'm tired of everything and everybody, from a moonlight picnic at Seepee to the blandishments of The Mussuck."

"Yes – that comes too, sooner or later. Have you nerve enough to make your bow yet?"

Mrs Hauksbee's mouth shut grimly. Then she laughed. "I think I see myself doing it. Big pink placards on the Mall: 'Mrs Hauksbee! Positively her last appearance on *any* stage! This is to give notice!' No more dances, no more rides, no more luncheons; no more theatricals with supper to follow; no more sparring with one's dearest, dearest friend; no more fencing with an inconvenient man who hasn't wit enough to clothe what he's pleased to call his sentiments in passable speech; no more parading of The Mussuck while Mrs Tarcass calls all round Simla, spreading horrible stories about me! No more of anything that is thoroughly wearying, abominable and detestable, but, all the same, makes life worth the having. Yes! I see it all! Don't interrupt, Polly, I'm inspired. A mauve and white striped 'cloud' round my venerable shoulders, a seat in the fifth row of the Gaiety, and both horses sold. Delightful vision! A comfortable armchair, situated in three different draughts, at every ballroom; and nice, large, sensible shoes for all the couples to stumble over as they go into the verandah! Then at supper. Can't you imagine the scene? The greedy mob gone away. Reluctant subaltern, pink all over, like a newly powdered baby – they really ought to tan subalterns before they are exported, Polly – sent back by the hostess to do his duty. Slouches up to me across the room, tugging at a glove two sizes too large for him – I hate a man who wears gloves like overcoats – and trying to look as if he'd thought of it from the first. 'May I ah-have the pleasure 'f takin' you'nt' supper?' Then I get up with a hungry smile; just like this."

"Lucy, how can you be so absurd?"

"And sweep out on his arm. So! After supper I shall go away early, you know, because I shall be afraid of catching cold. No one will look for my 'rickshaw. *Mine*, so please you! I shall stand, always with that mauve and white 'cloud' over my head, while the wet soaks into my dear, old, venerable feet and Tom swears and shouts for the 'rickshaw. Then home to bed at half-past eleven! Truly excellent life – helped out by the visits of the *Padri*, just fresh from burying somebody down below there." She pointed through the pines towards the Cemetery, and continued with vigorous dramatic gesture:

"Listen! I see it all – down, down even to the stays! Such stays! Six-eight a pair, Polly, with red flannel – or list is it? – that they put into the tops of those fearful things. I can draw you a picture of them."

"Lucy, for Heaven's sake, don't go waving your arms about in that idiotic manner! Recollect everyone can see you from the Mall."

"Let them see! They'll think I am rehearsing for *The Fallen Angel*. Look! There's The Mussuck. How badly he rides. There!"

She blew a kiss to the venerable Indian administrator with infinite grace.

"Now," she continued, "he'll be chaffed about that at the Club in the delicate manner these brutes of men affect, and the Hawley Boy will tell me all about it – softening the details for fear of shocking me. That boy is too good to live, Polly. I've serious thoughts of recommending him to throw up his Commission and go into the Church. In his present frame of mind he would obey me. Happy, happy child!"

"Never again," said Mrs Mallowe, with an affectation of indignation, "shall you tiffin here! Lucindy, your behaviour is scand'lus."

"All your fault," retorted Mrs Hauksbee, "for suggesting such a thing as my abdication. No! *Jamais* – Nevaire! I will act, dance, ride, frivol, talk scandal, dine out, and appropriate the legitimate captives of any woman I choose, until I d-r-r-op, or a better woman than I puts me to shame before all Simla – and it's dust and ashes in my mouth while I'm doing it!"

She dashed into the drawing room. Mrs Mallowe followed and put an arm round her waist.

"I'm *not!*" said Mrs Hauksbee defiantly, rummaging in the bosom of her dress for her handkerchief. "I've been dining out for the last ten nights, and rehearsing in the afternoons. You'd be tired yourself. It's only because I'm tired."

Mrs Mallowe did not at once overwhelm Mrs Hauksbee with spoken pity or ask her to lie down. She knew her friend too well. Handing her another cup of tea, she went on with the conversation.

"I've been through that too, dear," she said.

"I remember," said Mrs Hauksbee, a gleam of fun on her face. "In '84 wasn't it? You went out a great deal less next season."

Mrs Mallowe smiled in a superior and Sphinx-like fashion.

"I became an Influence," said she.

"Good gracious, child, you didn't join the Theosophists and kiss Buddha's big toe, did you? I tried to get into their set once, but they cast me out for a sceptic – without a chance of improving my poor little mind, too."

"No, I didn't Theosophilander. Jack says – "

"Never mind Jack. What did you do?"

"I made a lasting impression."

"So have I – for four months. But that didn't console me in the least. I hated the man. Will you stop smiling in that inscrutable way and tell me what you mean?"

Mrs Mallowe told.

"And – you – mean – to – say that it is absolutely Platonic on both sides?"

"Absolutely, or I should never have taken it up."

"And his last promotion was due to you?"

Mrs Mallowe nodded.

"And you warned him against the Topsham Girl?"

Another nod.

"And told him of Sir Dugald Delane's private Memo about him?"

A third nod.

"*Why?*"

"What a question to ask a woman! Because it amused me at first. I'm proud of my property now. If I live, he shall continue to be successful. Yes, I will put him upon the straight road to Knighthood, and everything else that a man values. The rest depends upon himself."

"Polly, you are a most extraordinary woman."

"Not in the least. I'm concentrated, that's all. You diffuse yourself, dear; and though all Simla knows your skill in managing a Team – "

"Can't you choose a prettier word?"

"Team of half-a-dozen, from The Mussuck to the Hawley Boy, you gain nothing by it. Not even amusement."

"And you?"

"Try my recipe. Take a man, not a boy, mind, but an almost mature, unattached man, and be his guide, philosopher and friend. You'll find it the most interesting occupation that you ever embarked on. It can be done – you needn't look like that – because I've done it."

"There's an element of danger about it that makes the notion attractive. I'll get such a man and say to him: 'Now there must be no flirtation. Do exactly what I tell you, profit by my instruction and counsels, and all will yet be well,' as Toole says. Is that the idea?"

"More or less," said Mrs Mallowe, with an unfathomable smile. "But be sure he understands that there must be no flirtation."

THE EDUCATION OF OTIS YEERE

Part II

SHOWING WHAT WAS BORN OF THE GREAT IDEA.

> "Dribble-dribble – trickle-trickle –
> What a lot of raw dust!
> My dollie's had an accident
> And out came all the sawdust!"
> *– Nursery Rhyme.*

So Mrs Hauksbee, in "The Foundry" which overlooks Simla Mall, sat at the feet of Mrs Mallowe and gathered wisdom. The end of the Conference was the Great Idea upon which Mrs Hauksbee so plumed herself.

"I warn you," said Mrs Mallowe, beginning to repent of her suggestion, "that the matter is not half so easy as it looks. Any woman – even the Topsham Girl – can catch a man, but very, very few know how to manage him when captured."

"My child," was the answer, "I've been a female St Simon Stylites looking down upon men for these – these years past. Ask The Mussuck whether I can manage them."

Mrs Hauksbee departed humming, *"I'll go to him and say to him, in manner most ironical"*. Mrs Mallowe laughed to herself. Then she grew suddenly sober. "I wonder whether I've done well in advising that amusement. Lucy's a clever woman, but a thought too mischievous where a man is concerned."

13

A week later, the two met at a Monday Pop. "Well?" said Mrs Mallowe.

"I've caught him!" said Mrs Hauksbee; her eyes dancing with merriment.

"Who is it, you mad woman? I'm sorry I ever spoke to you about it."

"Look between the pillars. In the third row; fourth from the end. You can see his face now. Look!"

"Otis Yeere! Of all the improbable people! I don't believe you."

"Hssh! Wait till Mrs Tarcass begins murdering Milton Wellings; and I'll tell you all about it. *S-s-ss!* There we are. That woman's voice always reminds me of an underground train coming into Earls Court with the brakes down. Now listen. It is really Otis Yeere."

"So I see, but it doesn't follow that he is your property."

"He *is*! By right of trove, as the barristers say. I found him, lonely and unbefriended, the very next night after our talk, at the Dugald Delane's dinner. I liked his eyes and I talked to him. Next day he called. Next day we went for a ride together, and today he's tied to my *'rickshaw* wheels hand and foot. You'll see when the concert's over. He doesn't know I'm here yet."

"Thank goodness you haven't chosen a boy. What are you going to do with him, assuming that you've got him?"

"Assuming, indeed! Does a woman – do I – ever make a mistake in that sort of thing? First" – Mrs Hauksbee ticked off the items ostentatiously on her daintily gloved fingers – "First, my dear, I shall dress him properly. At present his raiment is a disgrace, and he wears a dress shirt like a crumpled sheet of the *Pioneer*. Second, after I have made him presentable, I shall form his manners – his morals are above reproach."

"You seem to have discovered a great deal about him considering the shortness of your acquaintance."

"Surely you ought to know that the first proof a man gives of his interest in a woman is by talking to her about his own

14

sweet self. If the woman listens without yawning, he begins to like her. If she flatters the animal's vanity, he ends by adoring her."

"In some cases."

"Never mind the exceptions. I know which one you are thinking of. Thirdly, and lastly, after he is polished and made pretty, I shall, as you said, be his guide, philosopher and friend, and he shall become a success – as great a success as your friend. I always wondered how that man got on. Did The Mussuck come to you with the Civil List and, dropping on one knee – no, two knees, *à la* Gibbon – hand it to you and say: 'Adorable angel, choose your friend's appointment?' "

"Lucy, your long experiences of the Military department have demoralised you. One doesn't do that sort of thing on the Civil side."

"No disrespect meant to 'Jack's service,' my dear: I only asked for information. Give me three months, and see what changes I shall work in my prey."

"Go your own way, since you must. But I'm sorry that I was weak enough to suggest the amusement."

" 'I am all discretion and may be trusted to an in-fin-ite extent,' " quoted Mrs Hauksbee from *The Fallen Angel;* and the conversation ceased with Mrs Tarcass' last, long-drawn war whoop.

Her bitterest enemies, and she had many, could hardly accuse Mrs Hauksbee of wasting her time. Otis Yeere was one of those wandering "dumb" characters, foredoomed through life to be nobody's property. Ten years in Her Majesty's Bengal Civil Service, spent, for the most part, in undesirable Districts, had dowered him with little to be proud of, and nothing to give confidence. Old enough to have lost the first fine careless rapture that showers on the immature 'Stunt imaginary Commissionerships and Stars, and sends him into the collar with coltish earnestness and abandon; too young to be yet able to look back upon the progress he had made and thank Providence that under the conditions of today he had come even so far, he stood upon the dead centre of his career. And when a man stands still, he feels the slightest impulse from without. Fortune had ruled that Otis Yeere should be, for the first part of his service, one of the rank and file who are ground up in the wheels of the Administration; losing heart and soul, and mind and strength in the process. Until steam replaces manual power in the working of the Empire, there must always be this percentage – must always be the men who are used up, expended, in the mere mechanical routine. For these promotion is far off and the mill grind of every day very near and instant. The Secretariats know them only by name; they are not the picked men of the Districts, with the Divisions and Collectorates awaiting them. They are simply the rank and file – the food for fever – sharing with the *ryot* and the plough bullock the honour of being the plinth on which the State rests. The older ones have lost their aspirations; the younger are putting theirs aside with a sigh. Both learn to endure patiently until the end of the day. Twelve years in the rank and file, men say, will sap the hearts of the bravest and dull the wits of the most keen.

Out of this life Otis Yeere had fled for a few months; drifting, for the sake of a little masculine society, into Simla. When his leave was over he would return to his swampy, sour-green, undermanned District, the native Assistant, the native Doctor, the native Magistrate, the steaming, sweltering Station, the ill-kempt City, and the undisguised insolence of the Municipality that babbled away the lives of men. Life was cheap, however. The soil spawned humanity, as it bred frogs in the Rains, and the gap of the sickness of one season was filled to overflowing by the fecundity of the next. Otis was unfeignedly thankful to lay down his work for a little while and escape from the seething, whining, weakly hive, impotent to help itself but strong in its power to cripple, thwart and annoy the weary-eyed man who, by official irony, was said to be "in charge" of it.

"I knew there were women dowdies in Bengal. They come up here sometimes. But I didn't know that there were men dowds, too."

Then, for the first time, it occurred to Otis Yeere that his clothes were rather ancestral in appearance. It will be seen from the above that his friendship with Mrs Hauksbee had made great strides.

As that lady truthfully says, a man is never so happy as when he is talking about himself. From Otis Yeere's lips Mrs Hauksbee, before long, learned everything that she wished to know about the subject of her experiment; learned what manner of life he had led in what she vaguely called "those awful cholera districts"; learned, too, but this knowledge came later, what manner of life he had purposed to lead and what dreams he had dreamed in the year of grace '77, before the reality had knocked the heart out of him. Very pleasant are the shady bridle paths round Prospect Hill for the telling of confidences.

"Not yet," said Mrs Hauksbee to Mrs Mallowe. "Not yet. I must wait until the man is properly dressed, at least. Great Heavens, is it possible that he doesn't know what an honour it is to be taken up by *Me!*"

Mrs Hauksbee did not reckon false modesty as one of her failings.

"Always with Mrs Hauksbee!" murmured Mrs Mallowe, with her sweetest smile, to Otis. "Oh you men, you men! Here are our Punjabis growling because you've monopolised the nicest woman in Simla. They'll tear you to pieces on the Mall, some day, Mr Yeere."

Mrs Mallowe rattled downhill, having satisfied herself, by a glance through the fringe of her sunshade, of the effect of her words.

The shot went home. Of a surety Otis Yeere was somebody in this bewildering whirl of Simla. Had monopolised the nicest woman in it and the Punjabis were growling. The notion justified a mild glow of vanity. He had never regarded his acquaintance with Mrs Hauksbee as a matter for general interest.

The knowledge of envy was a pleasant feeling to the man of no account. It was intensified later in the day when a luncher at the Club said spitefully: "Well, for a debilitated Ditcher, Yeere, you are going it. Hasn't any kind friend told you that she's the most dangerous woman in Simla?"

Yeere chuckled and passed out. When, oh when, would his new clothes be ready? He descended into the Mall to enquire; and Mrs Hauksbee, coming over the Church Ridge in her *'rickshaw,* looked down upon him approvingly. "He's learning to carry himself as if he were a man, instead of a piece of furniture, and" – she screwed up her eyes to see the better through the sunlight – "he *is* a man when he holds himself like that. O blessed Conceit, what should we be without you?"

With the new clothes came a new stock of self-confidence. Otis Yeere discovered that he could enter a room without breaking into a gentle perspiration, and could cross one, even to talk to Mrs Hauksbee, as though rooms were meant to be crossed. He was, for the first time in nine years, proud of himself, and contented with his life, satisfied with his new clothes and rejoicing in the coveted friendship of Mrs Hauksbee.

"Conceit is what the poor fellow wants," she said in confidence to Mrs Mallowe. "I believe they must use Civilians to plough the fields with in Lower Bengal. You see I have to begin from the very beginning – haven't I? But you'll admit, won't you, dear, that he is immensely improved since I took him in hand. Only give me a little more time and he won't know himself."

Indeed, Yeere was rapidly beginning to forget what he had been. One of his own rank and file put the matter in a nutshell when he asked Yeere, in reference to nothing: "And who has been making you a Member of Council, lately? You carry the side of half-a-dozen of 'em."

"I-I'm awf'ly sorrow. I didn't mean it, you know," said Yeere apologetically.

"There'll be no holding you," continued the old stager grimly. "Climb down, Otis – climb down, or get all that beastly affectation knocked out of you with fever! Three thousand rupees a month wouldn't support it."

Yeere repeated the incident to Mrs Hauksbee. He had insensibly come to look upon her as his Frau Confessorin.

"And you apologised!" she said. "Oh shame! I hate a man who apologises. Never apologise for what your friend called 'side'. *Never!* It's a man's business to be insolent and overbearing until he meets with a stronger. Now, you bad boy, listen to me."

Simply and straightforwardly, as the 'rickshaw loitered round Jakko, Mrs Hauksbee preached to Otis Yeere the Great Gospel of Conceit, illustrating it with living subjects encountered during their Sunday afternoon stroll.

"Good gracious!" she concluded with the personal argument, "You'll apologise next for being my *attaché!*"

"Never!" said Otis Yeere. "That's another thing altogether. I shall always be – "

"What's coming?" thought Mrs Hauksbee.

"Proud of that," said Otis.

"Safe for the present," she said to herself.

"But I'm afraid I have grown conceited. Like Jeshurun, you know. When he waxed fat, then he kicked. It's the having no worry on one's mind and the Hill air, I suppose."

"Hill air, indeed!" said Mrs Hauksbee to herself. "He'd have been hiding in the Club till the last day of his leave, if I hadn't discovered him." Then aloud:

"Why shouldn't you be? You have every right to."

"I! Why?"

"Oh, hundreds of things. I'm not going to waste this lovely afternoon by explaining; but I know you have. What was that heap of manuscript you showed me about the grammar of the aboriginal – what's their names?"

19

"Gullals. A piece of nonsense. I've far too much work to do to bother over Gullals now. You should see my District. Come down with your husband some day and I'll show you round. Such a lovely place in the Rains! A sheet of water with the railway embankment and the snakes sticking out, and, in the summer, green flies and green squash. The people would die of fear if you shook a dogwhip at 'em. But they know you're forbidden to do that, so they conspire to make your life a burden to you. My District's worked by some man at Darjiling, on the strength of a native pleader's false reports. Oh, it's a heavenly place!"

Otis Yeere laughed bitterly.

"There's not the least necessity that you should stay in it. Why do you?"

"Because I must. How'm I to get out of it?"

"How! In a hundred and fifty ways. If there weren't so many people on the road, I'd like to box your ears. Ask, my dear Sir, ask! Look! There is young Hexarly with six years' service and half your talents. He asked for what he wanted and he got it. See, down by the Convent! There's McArthurson who has come to his present position by asking – sheer, downright asking – after he had pushed himself out of the rank and file. One man is as good as another in your service – believe me. I've seen Simla for more seasons than I care to think about. Do you suppose men are chosen for appointments because of their special fitness beforehand? You have all passed a high test – what do you call it? – in the beginning, and excepting the three or four who have gone altogether to the bad, you can all work. Asking does the rest. Call it cheek, call it insolence, call it anything you like, but *ask*! Men argue – yes, I know what men say – that a man, by the mere audacity of his request, must have some good in him. A weak man doesn't say: 'Give me this and that.' He whines: 'Why haven't I been given this and that?' If you were in the Army I should say learn to spin plates or play a tambourine with your toes. As it is – ask! You belong to a

Service that ought to be able to command the Channel fleet, or set a leg at twenty minutes' notice, and yet you hesitate over asking to escape from a squashy green district where you admit you are not master. Drop the Bengal Government altogether. Even Darjiling is a little, out-of-the-way hole. I was there once, and the rents were extortionate. Assert yourself. Get the Government of India to take you over. Try to get on the Frontier, where every man has a grand chance if he can trust himself. Go somewhere! Do something! You have twice the wits and three times the presence of the men up here, and, and" – Mrs Hauksbee paused for breath; then continued – "and in any way you look at it, you ought to. You who could go so far!"

"I don't know," said Yeere, rather taken aback by the unexpected eloquence. "I haven't such a good opinion of myself."

It was not strictly Platonic, but it was Policy. Mrs Hauksbee laid her hand lightly upon the ungloved paw that rested on the turned-back *'rickshaw* hood, and looking the man full in the face, said tenderly, almost too tenderly: "*I* believe in you if you mistrust yourself. Is that enough, my friend?"

"It is enough," answered Otis very solemnly.

He was silent for a long time, redreaming the dreams that he had dreamed eight years ago, but through them all ran, as sheet lightning through golden cloud, the light of Mrs Hauksbee's violet eyes.

Curious and impenetrable are the mazes of Simla life – the only existence in this desolate land worth the living. Gradually it went abroad among men and women, in the pauses between dance, play and Gymkhana, that Otis Yeere, the man with the newly lit light of self-confidence in his eyes, had "done something decent" in the wilds whence he came. He had brought an erring Municipality to reason, appropriated the funds on his own responsibility and saved the lives of hundreds. He knew more about the Gullals than any living man. Had a vast knowledge of the aboriginal tribes; was, in spite of his juniority, the greatest authority on the aboriginal Gullals. No one quite knew who or what the Gullals were till The Mussuck, who had been calling on Mrs Hauksbee, and prided himself upon picking people's brains for the good of the Government, explained they were a tribe of ferocious hillmen, somewhere near Sikkim, whose friendship even the Great Indian Empire would find it worth her while to secure. Now we know that Otis Yeere had showed Mrs Hauksbee his MS notes of six years' standing on these same Gullals. He had told her, too, how, sick and shaken with the fever their negligence had bred, crippled by the loss of his pet clerk, and savagely angry at the desolation in his charge, he had once damned the collective eyes of his "intelligent local board" for a set of pigs. Which act of "brutal and tyrannous oppression" won him a Reprimand Royal from the Bengal Government; but in the anecdote as amended for Northern consumption we find no record of this. Hence we are forced to conclude that Mrs Hauksbee edited his reminiscences before sowing them in idle ears, ready, as she well knew, to exaggerate good or evil. And Otis Yeere bore himself as befitted the hero of many tales.

You can talk to me when you don't fall into a brown study. Talk now, and talk your brightest and best," said Mrs Hauksbee.

Otis needed no spur. Look to a man who has the counsel of a woman of or above the world to back him. So long as he keeps his head, he can meet both sexes on equal ground – an advantage never intended by Providence, who fashioned Man on one day and Woman on another, in sign that neither should know more than a very little of the other's life. Such a man goes far, or, the counsel being withdrawn, collapses suddenly while his world seeks the reason.

Generalled by Mrs Hauksbee who, again, had all Mrs Mallowe's wisdom at her disposal, proud of himself and, in the end, believing in himself because he was believed in, Otis Yeere stood ready for any fortune that might befall, certain that it would be good. He would fight for his own hand, and intended that this second struggle should lead to better issue than the first helpless surrender of the bewildered junior.

What might have happened, it is impossible to say. This lamentable thing befell, bred directly by a statement of Mrs Hauksbee that she would spend the next season in Darjiling.

"Are you sure of that?" said Otis Yeere.

"Quite. We're writing about a house now."

Otis Yeere "stopped dead," as Mrs Hauksbee put it in discussing the relapse with Mrs Mallowe.

"He has behaved," she said angrily, "just like Captain Kerrington's pony – only Otis is a donkey – at the last Gymkhana. Planted his forefeet and refused to go on another step. Polly, my man's going to disappoint me. What shall I do?"

As a rule, Mrs Mallowe does not approve of staring, but on this occasion she opened her eyes to the utmost.

"You have managed cleverly so far," she said. "Speak to him and ask him what he means."

"I will – at tonight's dance."

"No-o, not at a dance," said Mrs Mallowe cautiously. "Men are never themselves quite at dances. Better wait till tomorrow morning."

"Nonsense. If he's going to revert in this insane way there isn't a day to lose. Are you going? No? Then sit up for me, there's a dear. I shan't stay longer than supper under any circumstances."

Mrs Mallowe waited through the evening, looking long and earnestly into the fire, and sometimes smiling to herself.

"Oh! Oh! Oh! The man's an idiot! A raving, positive idiot! I'm sorry I ever saw him!"

Mrs Hauksbee burst into Mrs Mallowe's house, at midnight, almost in tears.

"What in the world has happened?" said Mrs Mallowe, but her eyes showed that she had guessed an answer.

"Happened! Everything has happened! He was there. I went to him and said: 'Now, what does this nonsense mean?' Don't laugh, dear, I can't bear it. But you know what I mean I said. Then it was a square, and I sat it out with him and wanted an explanation, and *he* said – oh, I haven't patience with such idiots! You know what I said about going to Darjiling next year? It doesn't matter to me where I go. I'd have changed the Station and lost the rent to have saved this. He said, in so many words, that he wasn't going to try to work up any more because – because he would be shifted into a province away from Darjiling, and his own District, where these creatures are, is within a day's journey – "

"Ah-h-h!" said Mrs Mallowe, in the tone of one who has successfully tracked an obscure word through a large dictionary.

"Did you ever hear of anything so mad – so absurd? And he had the ball at his feet. He had only to kick it! I would have made him anything! Anything in the wide world. He could have gone to the world's end. I would have helped him. I made him, didn't I, Polly? Didn't I create that man? Doesn't he owe everything to me? And to reward me, just when everything was nicely arranged, by this lunacy that spoilt everything!"

"Very few men understand devotion thoroughly."

"Oh, Polly, don't laugh at me! I give men up from this hour. I could have killed him then and there. What *right* had this man – this Thing I had picked out of his filthy paddy fields – to make love to me?"

"He did that, did he?"

"He did. I don't remember half he said, I was so angry. Oh, but such a funny thing happened! I can't help laughing at it now, though I felt nearly ready to cry with rage. He raved and I stormed – I'm afraid we must have made an awful noise in our corner. Protect my character, dear, if it's all over Simla by tomorrow – and then he bobbed forward in the middle of this insanity – I firmly believe the man's demented – and kissed me."

"Morals above reproach," purred Mrs Mallowe.

"So they were – so they are! It was the most absurd kiss. I don't believe he'd ever kissed a woman in his life before. I threw my head back, and it was a sort of slidy, pecking dab, just on the end of the chin – here." Mrs Hauksbee tapped her rather masculine chin with her fan. "Then, of course, I was furiously angry and told him that he was no gentleman, and I was sorry I'd ever met him, and so on. He was crushed so easily that I couldn't be very angry. Then I came away straight to you."

"Was this before or after supper?"

"Oh, before – oceans before. Isn't it perfectly disgusting?"

"Let me think. I withhold judgement till tomorrow. Morning brings counsel."

But morning brought only a servant with a dainty bouquet of Annandale roses for Mrs Hauksbee to wear at the dance at Viceregal Lodge that night.

"He doesn't seem to be very penitent," said Mrs Mallowe. "What's the *billet-doux* in the centre?"

Mrs Hauksbee opened the neatly folded note – another accomplishment that she had taught Otis – read it and groaned tragically.

"Last wreck of a feeble intellect! Poetry! Is it his own, do you think? Oh, that I ever built my hopes on such a maudlin idiot!"

"No. It's a quotation from Mrs Browning, and, in view of the facts of the case, as Jack says, uncommonly well chosen. Listen:

> "Sweet thou hast trod on a heart
> Pass! There's a world full of men,
> And women as fair as thou art
> Must do such things now and then

25

> "Thou only hast stepped unaware –
>   Malice not one can impute,
> And why should a heart have been there,
>   In the way of a fair woman's foot?"

"I didn't – I didn't – I didn't!" said Mrs Hauksbee angrily, her eyes filling with tears. "There was no malice at all. Oh, it's *too* vexatious!"

"You've misunderstood the compliment," said Mrs Mallowe." He clears you completely and – ahem – I should think by this, that *he* has cleared completely too. My experience of men is, that when they begin to quote poetry they are going to flit. Like swans singing before they die, you know."

"Polly, you take my sorrows in a most unfeeling way."

"Do I? Is it so terrible? If he's hurt your vanity, I should say that you've done a certain amount of damage to his heart."

"Oh, you can never tell about a man!" said Mrs Hauksbee with deep scorn.

AT THE PIT'S MOUTH

"Men say it was a stolen tide –
    The Lord that sent it he knows all,
But in mine ear will aye abide
    The message that the bells let fall,
And awesome bells they were to me,
    That in the dark rang, 'Enderby'."

                                        – *Jean Ingelow*.

Once upon a time, there was a Man and his Wife and a
Tertium Quid.

All three were unwise, but the Wife was the unwisest. The
Man should have looked after his Wife, who should have
avoided the Tertium Quid, who, again, should have married a
wife of his own, after clean and open flirtations, to which
nobody can possibly object, round Jakko or Observatory Hill.
When you see a young man with his pony in a white lather, and
his hat on the back of his head flying downhill at fifteen miles
an hour to meet a girl who will be properly surprised to meet
him, you naturally approve of that young man and wish him
Staff appointments, and take an interest in his welfare, and, as
the proper time comes, give them sugar tongs or side saddles
according to your means and generosity.

The Tertium Quid flew downhill on horseback, but it was to
meet the Man's Wife; and when he flew uphill it was for the
same end. The Man was in the Plains, earning money for his
Wife to spend on dresses and four-hundred rupee bracelets, and

inexpensive luxuries of that kind. He worked very hard, and sent her a letter or a postcard daily. She also wrote to him daily, and said that she was longing for him to come up to Simla. The Tertium Quid used to lean over her shoulder and laugh as she wrote the notes. Then the two would ride to the Post Office together.

Now, Simla is a strange place, and its customs are peculiar; nor is any man who has not spent at least ten seasons there qualified to pass judgement on circumstantial evidence, which is the most untrustworthy in the Courts. For these reasons, and for others which need not appear, I decline to state positively whether there was anything irretrievably wrong in the relations between the Man's Wife and the Tertium Quid. If there was, and hereon you must form your own opinion, it was the Man's Wife's fault. She was kittenish in her manners, wearing generally an air of soft and fluffy innocence. But she was deadlily learned and evil-instructed; and, now and again, when the mask dropped, men saw this, shuddered and – almost drew back. Men are occasionally particular, and the least particular men are always the most exacting.

Simla is eccentric in its fashion of treating friendships. Certain attachments which have set and crystallised through half-a-dozen seasons acquire almost the sanctity of the marriage bond, and are revered as such. Again, certain attachments equally old, and to all appearances, equally venerable, never seem to win any recognised official status; while a chance-sprung acquaintance, not two months old, steps into the place which by right belongs to the senior. There is no law reducible to print which regulates these affairs.

Some people have a gift which secures them infinite toleration, and others have not. The Man's Wife had not. If she looked over the garden wall, for instance, women taxed her with stealing their husbands. She complained pathetically that she was not allowed to choose her own friends. When she put up her big white muff to her lips and gazed over it and under her eyebrows at you as she said this thing, you felt that she had been infamously misjudged, and that all the other women's instincts were all wrong: which was absurd. She was not allowed to own the Tertium Quid in peace; and was so strangely constructed that she would not have enjoyed peace had she been so permitted. She preferred some semblance of intrigue to cloak even her most commonplace actions.

After two months of riding, first round Jakko, then Elysium, then Summer Hill, then Observatory Hill, then under Jutogh, and lastly up and down the Cart Road as far as the Tara Devi gap in the dusk, she said to the Tertium Quid: "Frank, people say we are too much together, and people are so horrid."

The Tertium Quid pulled his moustache and replied that horrid people were unworthy of the consideration of nice people.

"But they have done more than talk – they have written – written to my hubby – I'm sure of it," said the Man's Wife, and she pulled a letter from her husband out of her saddle pocket and gave it to the Tertium Quid.

It was an honest letter, written by an honest man, then stewing in the Plains on two hundred rupees a month (for he allowed his wife eight hundred and fifty), and in a silk banian and cotton trousers. It said that perhaps she had not thought of the unwisdom of allowing her name to be so generally coupled with the Tertium Quid's; that she was too much of a child to understand the dangers of that sort of thing; that he, her husband, was the last man in the world to interfere jealously with her little amusements and interests, but that it would be better were she to drop the Tertium Quid quietly and for her husband's sake. The letter was sweetened with many pretty little pet names, and it amused the Tertium Quid considerably. He and She laughed over it, so that you, fifty yards away, could see their shoulders shaking while the horses slouched along side by side.

Their conversation was not worth reporting. The upshot of it was that, next day, no one saw the Man's Wife and the Tertium Quid together. They had both gone down to the Cemetery, which, as a rule, is only visited officially by the inhabitants of Simla.

A Simla funeral with the clergyman riding, the mourners riding, and the coffin creaking as it swings between the bearers, is one of the most depressing things on this earth, particularly when the procession passes under the wet, dank dip beneath the Rockcliffe Hotel, where the sun is shut out, and all the hill streams are wailing and weeping together as they go down the valleys.

Occasionally folk tend the graves, but we in India shift and are transferred so often that, at the end of the second year the dead have no friends – only acquaintances who are far too busy amusing themselves up the hill to attend to old partners. The idea of using a Cemetery as a rendezvous is distinctly a feminine one. A man would have said simply: "Let people talk. We'll go down the Mall." A woman is made differently, especially if she be such a woman as the Man's Wife. She and the Tertium Quid enjoyed each other's society among the graves of men and women that they had known and danced with aforetime.

They used to take a big horse blanket and sit on the grass a little to the left of the lower end, where there is a dip in the ground, and where the occupied graves die out and the vacant ones are made ready. Any self-respecting Indian Cemetery keeps half-a-dozen graves permanently open for contingencies and incidental wear and tear. In the Hills these are more usually baby's size, because children who come up weakened and sick from the Plains below often succumb to the effects of the Rains in the Hills, or get pneumonia from their *ayahs* taking them through damp pinewoods after sunset. In Cantonments, of course, the man's size is more in request; these arrangements varying with the climate and population.

One day when the Man's Wife and the Tertium Quid had just arrived in the Cemetery, they saw some coolies breaking ground. They had marked out a full-size grave, and the Tertium Quid asked them whether any *Sahib* was sick. They said that they did not know; but it was an order that they should dig a *Sahib*'s grave.

"Work away," said the Tertium Quid, "and let's see how it's done."

The coolies worked away, and the Man's Wife and the Tertium Quid watched and talked for a couple of hours while the grave was being deepened. Then a coolie, taking the earth in baskets as it was thrown up, jumped over the grave.

"That's queer," said the Tertium Quid. "Where's my ulster?"

"What's queer?" said the Man's Wife.

"I have got a chill down my back – just as if a goose had walked over my grave."

"Why do you look at the horror, then?" said the Man's Wife. "Let us go."

The Tertium Quid stood at the head of the grave, and stared without answering for a space. Then he said, dropping a pebble down: "It is nasty – and cold: horribly cold. I don't think I shall come to the Cemetery anymore. I don't think grave-digging is cheerful."

The two talked and agreed that the Cemetery was depressing. They also arranged for a ride next day, out from the Cemetery through the Mashobra Tunnel up to Fagoo and back, because all the world was going to a garden party at Viceregal Lodge, and all the people of Mashobra would go too.

Coming up the Cemetery road, the Tertium Quid's horse tried to bolt uphill, being tired with standing so long, and managed to strain a back sinew.

"I shall have to take the mare tomorrow," said the Tertium Quid, "and she will stand nothing heavier than a snaffle."

They made their arrangements to meet in the Cemetery, after allowing all the Mashobra people time to pass into Simla. That night it rained heavily, and, next day, when the Tertium Quid came to the trysting place, he saw that the new grave had a foot of water in it, the ground being a tough and sour clay.

"Jove! That looks beastly," said the Tertium Quid. "Fancy being boarded up and dropped into that well!"

They then started off to Fagoo, the mare playing with the snaffle and picking her way as though she were shod with satin, and the sun shining divinely. The road below Mashobra to Fagoo is officially styled the Himalayan-Thibet Road; but in spite of its name it is not much more than six feet wide in most places, and the drop into the valley below may be anything between one and two thousand feet.

"Now we're going to Thibet," said the Man's Wife merrily as the horses drew near to Fagoo. She was riding on the cliff side.

"Into Thibet," said the Tertium Quid, "ever so far from people who say horrid things, and hubbies who write stupid letters. With you – to the end of the world!"

A coolie carrying a log of wood came round a corner and the mare went wide to avoid him – forefeet in and haunches out, as a sensible mare should go.

"To the world's end," said the Man's Wife, and looked unspeakable things over her near shoulder at the Tertium Quid.

He was smiling, but, while she looked, the smile froze stiff as it were, on his face, and changed to a nervous grin – the sort of grin that men wear when they are not quite easy in their saddles. The mare seemed to be sinking by the stern, and her nostrils cracked while she was trying to realise what was happening. The rain of the previous night had rotted the dropside of the Himalayan–Thibet Road, and it was giving way under her. "What are you doing?" said the Man's Wife. The Tertium Quid gave no answer. He grinned nervously and set his spurs into the mare who rapped with her forefeet on the road, and the struggle began. The Man's Wife screamed, "Oh Frank, get off!"

But the Tertium Quid was glued to the saddle – his face blue and white – and he looked into the Man's Wife's eyes. Then the Man's Wife clutched at the mare's head and caught her by the nose instead of the bridle. The mare threw up her head and went down with a scream, the Tertium Quid upon her, and the nervous grin still set on his face.

The Man's Wife heard the tinkle-tinkle of little stones and loose earth falling off the roadway, and the sliding roar of man and horse descending. Then everything was quiet, and she called on Frank to leave his mare and walk up. But Frank did not answer. He was underneath the mare, nine hundred feet down the cliff, spoiling a patch of Indian corn.

As the revellers came back from Viceregal Lodge in the mists of the evening, they met a temporarily insane woman, on a wild horse, swinging round the corners, with her eyes and her mouth open, and her head like the head of a Medusa. She was stopped by a man at the risk of his life, and taken out of the saddle, a limp heap, and put on the bank to explain herself. This wasted twenty minutes, and then she was sent home in a lady's 'rickshaw, still with her mouth open and her hands picking at her riding gloves.

She was in bed for the following three days, which were rainy; so she missed attending the funeral of the Tertium Quid, who was lowered into eighteen inches of water, instead of the twelve to which he had first objected.

A WAYSIDE COMEDY

"Because to every purpose there is time and judgement;
therefore the misery of man is great upon him."

– Eccl. viii. 6.

Fate and the Government of India have turned the Station
of Kashima into a prison; and, because there is no help for
the poor souls who are now lying there in torment I write this
story, praying that the Government of India may be moved to
scatter the European population to the Four Winds.

Kashima is bounded on all sides by the rock-tipped circle of
the Dosehri hills. In Spring it is ablaze with roses; in Summer
the roses die and the hot winds blow from the hills; in Autumn,
the white mists from the swamps cover the place as with water,
and in Winter the frosts nip everything young and tender to
earth level. There is but one view in Kashima – a stretch of
perfectly flat pasture and ploughland, running up to the grey-
blue scrub of the Dosehri hills.

There are no amusements except snipe and tiger-shooting;
but the tigers have been long since hunted from their lairs in
the rock caves, and the snipe only come once a year. Narkarra
– one hundred and forty-three miles by road – is the nearest
station to Kashima. But Kashima never goes to Narkarra,
where there are at least twelve English people. It stays within
the circle of the Dosehri hills.

All Kashima acquits Mrs Vansuythen of any intention to do harm; but all Kashima knows that she, and she alone, brought about their pain.

Boulte, the Engineer, Mrs Boulte, and Captain Kurrell know this. They are the English population of Kashima, if we except Major Vansuythen, who is of no importance whatever, and Mrs Vansuythen, who is the most important of all.

You must remember, though you will not understand, that all laws weaken in a small and hidden community where there is no public opinion. If the Israelites had been only a ten-tent camp of gipsies, their Headman would never have taken the trouble to climb a hill and bring down the lithographed edition of the Decalogue, and a great deal of trouble would have been avoided. When a man is absolutely alone in a Station he runs a certain risk of falling into evil ways. This risk is multiplied by every addition to the population up to twelve – the Jury number. After that, fear and consequent restraint begin, and human action becomes less grotesquely jerky.

There was deep peace in Kashima till Mrs Vansuythen arrived. She was a charming woman, every one said so everywhere; and she charmed everyone. In spite of this, or, perhaps, because of this, since Fate is so maliciously perverse, she cared only for one man, and he was Major Vansuythen. Had she been plain or stupid, this matter would have been intelligible to Kashima. But she was a fair woman, with very still, grey eyes, the colour of a lake just before the light of the sun touches it. No man who had seen those eyes could, later on, explain what fashion of woman she was to look upon. The eyes dazzled him. Her own sex said that she was "not bad looking, but spoilt by pretending to be so grave". And yet, her gravity was natural. It was not her habit to smile. She merely went through life, looking at those who passed; and the women objected while the men fell down and worshipped.

She knows and is deeply sorry for the evil she has done to Kashima, but Major Vansuythen cannot understand why Mrs

Boulte does not drop in to afternoon tea at least three times a week. "When there are only two women in one Station, they ought to see a great deal of each other," says Major Vansuythen.

Long and long before ever Mrs Vansuythen came out of those faraway places where there is society and amusement, Kurrell had discovered that Mrs Boulte was the one woman in the world for him and – you dare not blame them. Kashima was as out of the world as Heaven or the other Place, and the Dosehri hills kept their secret well. Boulte had no concern in the matter. He went into camp for a fortnight at a time. He was a hard, heavy man, and neither Mrs Boulte nor Kurrell pitied him. They possessed all Kashima and each other for their very, very own; and Kashima was the Garden of Eden in those days. When Boulte returned from his wanderings, he would slap Kurrell between the shoulders, and call him "old fellow," and the three would dine together. Kashima was happy then, for the judgement of God seemed almost as distant as Narkarra or the railway that ran down to the sea. But the Government, which is the servant of Fate, sent Major Vansuythen to Kashima, and with him came his wife.

The etiquette of Kashima is much the same as that of a desert island. When a stranger is cast away there all hands go down to the shore to make him welcome. Kashima assembled at the masonry platform close to the Narkarra Road, and spread tea for the Vansuythens. That ceremony was reckoned a formal call, and made them free of the Station, its rights and privileges. When the Vansuythens were settled down, they gave a tiny house-warming to all Kashima; and that made all Kashima free of their house, according to the immemorial usage of the Station.

Then the Rains came, when no one could go into camp, and the Narkarra Road was washed away by the Kasun river, and in the cup-like pastures of Kashima the cattle waded knee-deep.

The clouds dropped down from the Dosehri hills and covered all.

At the end of the Rains, Boulte's manner towards his wife changed and became demonstratively affectionate. They had been married twelve years, and the change startled Mrs Boulte who hated her husband with the hate of a woman who has met with nothing but kindness from her mate, and, in the teeth of this kindness, has done him a great wrong. Moreover, she had her own trouble to fight with – her watch to keep over her own property, Kurrell. For two months the Rains had hidden the Dosehri hills and many other things beside: but, when they lifted, they showed Mrs Boulte that her man among men, her Ted – for she called him Ted in the old days when Boulte was out of earshot – was slipping the links of the allegiance.

"The Vansuythen Woman has taken him," Mrs Boulte said to herself; and when Boulte was away, wept over her belief, in the face of the over-vehement blandishments of Ted. Sorrow in Kashima is as fortunate as Love, in that there is nothing to weaken it save the flight of Time. Mrs Boulte had never breathed her suspicion to Kurrell because she was not certain; and her nature led her to be very certain before she took steps in any direction. That is why she behaved as she did.

Boulte came into the house one evening and leaned against the doorposts of the drawing room, chewing his moustache. Mrs Boulte was putting some flowers into a vase. There is a pretence of civilisation even in Kashima.

"Little woman," said Boulte quietly, "do you care for me?"

"Immensely," said she, with a laugh. "Can you ask it?"

"But I'm serious," said Boulte. "Do you care for me?"

Mrs Boulte dropped the flowers, and turned round quickly. "Do you want an honest answer?"

"Ye-es. I've asked for it."

Mrs Boulte spoke in a low, even voice for five minutes, very distinctly, that there might be no misunderstanding her meaning. When Samson broke the pillars of Gaza, he did a little thing, and one not to be compared to the deliberate pulling down of a woman's homestead about her own ears. There was no wise female friend to advise Mrs Boulte, the singularly cautious wife, to hold her hand. She struck at Boulte's heart, because her own was sick with suspicion of Kurrell, and worn out with the long strain of watching alone through the Rains. There was no plan or purpose in her speaking. The sentences made themselves; and Boulte listened, leaning against the doorpost with his hands in his pockets. When all was over, and Mrs Boulte began to breathe through her nose before breaking out into tears, he laughed and stared straight in front of him at the Dosehri hills.

"Is that all?" he said. "Thanks, I only wanted to know, you know?"

"What are you going to do?" said the woman, between her sobs.

"Do! Nothing. What should I do? Kill Kurrell or send you Home, or apply for leave to get a divorce? It's two days' ride into Narkarra." He laughed again and went on: "I'll tell you what you can do. You can ask Kurrell to dinner tomorrow – no, on Thursday, that will allow you time to pack – and you can bolt with him. I give you my word I won't follow."

He took up his helmet and went out of the room, and Mrs Boulte sat till the moonlight streaked the floor, thinking and thinking and thinking. She had done her best upon the spur of the moment to pull the house down; but it would not fall. Moreover, she could not understand her husband, and she was afraid. Then the folly of her useless truthfulness struck her, and she was ashamed to write to Kurrell, saying: "I have gone mad and told everything. My husband says that I am free to elope with you. Get horses for Thursday, and we will fly after dinner." There was a cold-bloodedness about that procedure which did not appeal to her. So she sat still in her own house and thought.

39

At dinner time Boulte came back from his walk, white and worn and haggard, and the woman was touched at his distress. As the evening wore on, she muttered some expression of sorrow, something approaching to contrition. Boulte came out of a brown study and said: "Oh *that*! I wasn't thinking about that. By the way, what does Kurrell say to the elopement?"

"I haven't seen him," said Mrs Boulte. "Good God, is that all?"

But Boulte was not listening, and her sentence ended in a gulp.

The next day brought no comfort to Mrs Boulte, for Kurrell did not appear, and the new life that she, in the five minutes' madness of the previous evening, had hoped to build out of the ruins of the old, seemed to be no nearer.

Boulte ate his breakfast, advised her to see her Arab pony fed in the verandah, and went out. The morning wore through, and at midday the tension became unendurable. Mrs Boulte could not cry. She had finished her crying in the night; and now she did not want to be left alone. Perhaps the Vansuythen Woman would talk to her; and, since talking opens the heart, perhaps there might be some comfort to be found in her company. She was the only other woman in the Station.

In Kashima there are no regular calling hours. Everyone can drop in upon everyone else at pleasure. Mrs Boulte put on a big hat, and walked across to the Vansuythen's house to borrow the *Queen*. The two compounds touched, and instead of going up the drive, she crossed through the gap in the cactus hedge, entering the house from the back. As she passed through the dining-room, she heard, behind the curtain that cloaked the drawing-room door, her husband's voice, saying:

"But on my honour! On my Soul and Honour, I tell you she doesn't care for me. She told me so last night. I would have told you then if Vansuythen hadn't been with you. If it is for *her* sake that you'll have nothing to say to me, you can make your mind easy. It's Kurrell –"

"What?" said Mrs Vansuythen, with an hysterical little laugh. "Kurrell! Oh it can't be! You two must have made some horrible mistake. Perhaps you – you lost your temper, or misunderstood, or something. Things can't be as wrong as you say."

Mrs Vansuythen had shifted her defence to avoid the man's pleading, and was desperately trying to keep him to a side issue.

"There must be some mistake," she insisted, "and it can be all put right again."

Boulte laughed grimly.

"It can't be Captain Kurrell! He told me that he had never taken the least – the least interest in your wife, Mr Boulte. Oh *do* listen! He said he had not. He swore he had not," said Mrs Vansuythen.

The curtain rustled, and the speech was cut short by the entry of a little, thin woman, with big rings round her eyes. Mrs Vansuythen stood up with a gasp.

"What was that you said?" asked Mrs Boulte. "Never mind that man. What did Ted say to you? What did he say to you? What did he say to you?"

Mrs Vansuythen sat down helplessly on the sofa, overborne by the trouble of her questioner.

"He said – I can't remember exactly what he said – but I understood him to say – that is – But, really, Mrs Boulte, isn't it rather a strange question?"

"Will you tell me what he said?" repeated Mrs Boulte.

Even a tiger will fly before a bear robbed of her whelps, and Mrs Vansuythen was only an ordinarily good woman.

She began in a sort of desperation: "Well, he said that he never cared for you at all, and, of course, there was not the least reason why he should have, and – and – that was all."

"You said he *swore* he had not cared for me. Was that true?"

"Yes," said Mrs Vansuythen very softly.

Mrs Boulte wavered for an instant where she stood, and then fell forward fainting.

"What did I tell you?" said Boulte, as though the conversation had been unbroken. "You can see for yourself. She cares for *him*." The light began to break into his dull mind, and he went on – "And he – what was he saying to you?"

But Mrs Vansuythen, with no heart for explanations or impassioned protestations, was kneeling over Mrs Boulte.

"Oh you brute!" she cried. "Are all men like this? Help me to get her into my room – and her face is cut against the table. Oh, will you be quiet, and help me to carry her? I hate you, and I hate Captain Kurrell. Lift her up carefully and now – go! Go away!"

Boulte carried his wife into Mrs Vansuythen's bedroom and departed before the storm of that lady's wrath and disgust, impenitent and burning with jealousy. Kurrell had been making love to Mrs Vansuythen – would do Vansuythen as great a wrong as he had done Boulte who caught himself considering whether Mrs Vansuythen would faint if she discovered that the man she loved had forsworn her.

In the middle of these meditations, Kurrell came cantering along the road and pulled up with a cheery, "Good mornin'. Been mashing Mrs Vansuythen as usual, eh? Bad thing for a sober, married man, that. What will Mrs Boulte say?"

Boulte raised his head and said slowly: "Oh you liar."

Kurrell's face changed. "What's that?" he asked quickly.

"Nothing much," said Boulte. "Has my wife told you that you two are free to go off whenever you please? She has been good enough to explain the situation to me. You've been a true friend to me, Kurrell, old man, haven't you?"

Kurrell groaned, and tried to frame some sort of idiotic sentence about being willing to give "satisfaction". But his interest in the woman was dead, had died out in the Rains, and, mentally, he was abusing her for her amazing indiscretion. It would have been so easy to have broken off the affair gently and by degrees, and now he was saddled with – Boulte's voice recalled him.

"I don't think I should get any satisfaction from killing you, and I'm pretty sure you'd get none from killing me."

Then in a querulous tone, ludicrously disproportioned to his wrongs, Boulte added:

"Seems rather a pity that you haven't the decency to keep to the woman, now you've got her. You've been a true friend to *her* too, haven't you?"

Kurrell stared long and gravely. The situation was getting beyond him.

"What do you mean?" he said.

Boulte answered, more to himself than the questioner: "My wife came over to Mrs Vansuythen's just now; and it seems, you'd been telling Mrs Vansuythen that you'd never cared for Emma. I suppose you lied, as usual. What had Mrs Vansuythen to do with you, or you with her? Try to speak the truth for once in a way."

Kurrell took the double insult without wincing, and replied by another question: "Go on. What happened?"

"Emma fainted," said Boulte simply. "But, look here, what had you been saying to Mrs Vansuythen?"

Kurrell laughed. Mrs Boulte had, with unbridled tongue, made havoc of his plans; and he could at least retaliate by hurting the man in whose eyes he was humiliated and shown dishonourable.

"Said to her? What does a man tell a lie like that for? I suppose I said pretty much what you've said, unless I'm a good deal mistaken."

"I spoke the truth," said Boulte, again more to himself than Kurrell. "Emma told me she hated me. She has no right in me."

"No! I suppose not. You're only her husband, y'know. And what did Mrs Vansuythen say after you had laid your disengaged heart at her feet?"

Kurrell felt almost virtuous as he put the question.

"I don't think that matters," Boulte replied; "and it doesn't concern you."

"But it does! I tell you it does," began Kurrell shamelessly.

The sentence was cut by a roar of laughter from Boulte's lips. Kurrell was silent for an instant, and then he, too, laughed – laughed long and loudly, rocking in his saddle. It was an unpleasant sound – the mirthless mirth of these men on the long, white line of the Narkarra road. There were no strangers in Kashima, or they might have thought that captivity within the Dosehri hills had driven half the European population mad. The laughter stopped abruptly. Kurrell was the first to speak.

"Well, what are you going to do?"

Boulte looked up the road, and at the hills. "Nothing," said he quietly. "What's the use? It's too ghastly for anything. We must let the old life go on. I can only call you a hound and a liar, and I can't go on calling you names for ever. Besides which, I don't feel that I'm much better. We can't get out of this place, y'know. What *is* there to do?"

Kurrell looked round the rat pit of Kashima and made no reply. The injured husband took up the wondrous tale.

"Ride on, and speak to Emma if you want to. God knows *I* don't care what you do."

He walked forward, and left Kurrell gazing blankly after him. Kurrell did not ride on either to see Mrs Boulte or Mrs Vansuythen. He sat in his saddle and thought, while his pony grazed by the roadside.

The whir of approaching wheels roused him. Mrs Vansuythen was driving home Mrs Boulte, white and wan, with a cut on her forehead.

"Stop, please," said Mrs Boulte, "I want to speak to Ted."

Mrs Vansuythen obeyed, but as Mrs Boulte leaned forward, putting her hand upon the splashboard of the dog cart, Kurrell spoke.

"I've seen your husband, Mrs Boulte."

There was no necessity for any further explanation. The man's eyes were fixed, not upon Mrs Boulte but her companion. Mrs Boulte saw the look.

"Speak to him!" she pleaded turning to the woman at her side. "Oh, speak to him! Tell him what you told me just now. Tell him you hate him! Tell him you hate him."

She bent forward and wept bitterly, while the groom, decorously impassive, went forward to hold the horse. Mrs Vansuythen turned scarlet and dropped the rein. She wished to be no party to such an unholy explanation.

"I've nothing to do with it," she began coldly, but Mrs Boulte's sobs overcame her and she addressed herself to the man. "I don't know what I am to say, Captain Kurrell. I don't know what I can call you. I think you've – you've behaved abominably, and she has cut her forehead terribly against the table."

"It doesn't hurt. It isn't anything," said Mrs Boulte feebly. "That doesn't matter. Tell him what you told me. Say you don't care for him. Oh, Ted, won't you believe her?"

"Mrs Boulte has made me understand that you were – that you were fond of her once upon a time," went on Mrs Vansuythen.

"Well!" said Kurrell brutally. "It seems to me that Mrs Boulte had better be fond of her own husband first."

"Stop!" said Mrs Vansuythen. "Hear me first. I don't care – I don't want to know anything about you and Mrs Boulte; but I want you to know that I hate you, that I think you are a cur, and that I'll never, never speak to you again. Oh, I don't dare to say what I think of you, you — man!"

"I want to speak to Ted," moaned Mrs Boulte, but the dog cart rattled on, and Kurrell was left on the road, shamed and boiling with wrath against Mrs Boulte.

He waited till Mrs Vansuythen was driving back to her own house, and, she being freed from the embarrassment of Mrs Boulte's presence, learned for the second time a truthful opinion of himself and his actions.

In the evenings it was the wont of all Kashima to meet at the platform on the Narkarra road, to drink tea and discuss the trivialities of the day. Major Vansuythen and his wife found themselves alone at the gathering place for almost the first time in their remembrance; and the cheery Major, in the teeth of his wife's remarkably reasonable suggestion that the rest of the Station might be sick, insisted upon driving round to the two bungalows and unearthing the population.

"Sitting in the twilight!" said he, with great indignation to the Boultes. "That'll never do! Hang it all, we're one family here! You must come out, and so must Kurrell. I'll make him bring his banjo."

So great is the power of honest simplicity and a good digestion over guilty consciences that all Kashima did turn out, even down to the banjo; and the Major embraced the company in one expansive grin. As he grinned Mrs Vansuythen raised her eyes for an instant and looked at Kashima. Her meaning was clear. Major Vansuythen would never know anything. He was to be the outsider in that happy family whose cage was the Dosehri hills.

"You're singing villainously out of tune, Kurrell," said the Major, truthfully. "Pass me that banjo."

And he sang in excruciating-wise till the stars came out and Kashima went to dinner.

That was the beginning of the New Life of Kashima – the life that Mrs Boulte made when her tongue was loosened in the twilight.

Mrs Vansuythen has never told the Major; and since he insists upon the maintenance of a burdensome geniality, she has been compelled to break her vow of not speaking to Kurrell. This speech, which must of necessity preserve the semblance of politeness and interest, serves admirably to keep alight the flame of jealousy and dull hatred in Boulte's bosom, as it awakens the same passions in his wife's heart. Mrs Boulte hates Mrs Vansuythen because she has taken Ted from her, and, in some curious fashion, hates her because Mrs Vansuythen – and here the wife's eyes see far more clearly than the husband's – detests Ted. And Ted – that gallant Captain and honourable man – knows now that it is possible to hate a woman once loved, even to the verge of wishing to silence her for ever with blows. Above all, is he shocked that Mrs Boulte cannot see the error of her ways.

Boulte and he go out tiger-shooting together in amity and all good friendship. Boulte has put their relationship on a most satisfactory footing.

"You're a blackguard," he says to Kurrell, "and I've lost any self-respect I may ever have had; but when you're with me, I can feel certain that you are not with Mrs Vansuythen, or making Emma miserable."

Kurrell endures anything that Boulte may say to him. Sometimes they are away for three days together, and then the Major insists upon his wife going over to sit with Mrs Boulte; although Mrs Vansuythen has repeatedly vowed that she prefers her husband's company to any in the world. From the way in which she clings to him, she would certainly appear to be speaking the truth.

But of course, as the Major says, "in a little Station we must all be friendly."

THE HILL OF ILLUSION

"What rendered vain their deep desire?
A God, a God their severance ruled,
And bade between their shores to be
The unplumbed, salt, estranging sea."

– M Arnold.

HE. – Tell your men not to hurry so, dear. They forget I'm fresh from the Plains.

SHE. – Sure proof that *I* have not been going out with anyone. Yes, they are an untrained crew. Where do we go?

HE. – As usual – to the world's end. No, Jakko.

SHE. – Have your pony led after you, then. It's a long round.

HE. – And for the last time, thank Heaven!

SHE. – Do you mean that still? I didn't dare to write to you about it – all these months.

HE. – Mean it! I've been shaping my affairs to that end since Autumn. What makes you speak as though it had occurred to you for the first time?

SHE. – I? Oh! I don't know. I've had long enough to think, too.

HE. – And you've changed your mind?

SHE. – No. You ought to know that I am a miracle of constancy. What are your – arrangements?

HE. – *Ours,* Sweetheart, please.

SHE. – Ours, be it then. My poor boy, how the prickly heat has marked your forehead! Have you ever tried sulphate of copper in water?

HE. – It'll go away in a day or two up here. The arrangements are simple enough. Tonga in the early morning – reach Kalka at twelve – Umballa at seven – down, straight by night-train, to Bombay, and then the steamer of the 21st for Rome. That's my idea. The Continent and Sweden – a ten-week honeymoon.

SHE. – Ssh! Don't talk of it in that way. It makes me afraid. Guy, how long have we two been insane?

HE. – Seven months and fourteen days. I forget the odd hours exactly, but I'll think.

SHE. – I only wanted to see if you remembered. Who are those two on the Blessington Road?

HE. – Eabrey and the Penner woman. What do they matter to us? Tell me everything that you've been doing and saying and thinking.

SHE. – Doing little, saying less, and thinking a great deal. I've hardly been out at all.

HE. – That was wrong of you. You haven't been moping?

SHE. – Not very much. Can you wonder that I'm disinclined for amusement?

HE. – Frankly, I do. Where was the difficulty?

SHE. – In this only. The more people I know and the more I'm known here, the wider spread will be the news of the crash when it comes. I don't like that.

HE. – Nonsense. We shall be out of it.

SHE. – You think so?

HE. – I'm sure of it, if there is any power in steam or horseflesh to carry us away. Ha! Ha!

SHE. – And the *fun* of the situation comes in – where, my Lancelot?

HE. – Nowhere, Guinevere. I was only thinking of something.

50

SHE. – They say men have a keener sense of humour than women. Now *I* was thinking of the scandal.

HE. – Don't think of anything so ugly. We shall be beyond it.

SHE. – It will be there all the same – in the mouths of Simla – telegraphed over India, and talked of at the dinners – and when He goes out they will stare at Him to see how He takes it. And we shall be dead, Guy dear – dead and cast into the outer darkness where there is –

HE. – Love at least. Isn't that enough?

SHE. – I have said so.

HE. – And you think so still?

SHE. – What do you think?

HE. – What have I done? It means equal ruin to me, as the world reckons it – outcasting, the loss of my appointment, breaking off my life's work. I pay my price.

SHE. – And are you so much above the world that you can afford to pay it? Am I?

HE. – My Divinity – what else?

SHE. – A very ordinary woman I'm afraid, but, so far, respectable. – How d'you do, Mrs Middleditch? Your husband? I think he's riding down to Annandale with Colonel Statters? Yes, isn't it divine after the rain? – Guy, how long am I to be allowed to bow to Mrs Middleditch? Till the 17th?

HE. – Frowsy Scotchwoman! What is the use of bringing her into the discussion? You were saying?

SHE. – Nothing. Have you ever seen a man hanged?

HE. – Yes. Once.

SHE. – What was it for?

HE. – Murder, of course.

SHE. – Murder. Is that so great a sin after all? I wonder how he felt before the drop fell.

HE. – I don't think he felt much. What a gruesome little woman it is this evening! You're shivering. Put on your cape, dear.

SHE. – I think I will. Oh! Look at the mist coming over Sanjaoli; and I thought we should have sunshine on the Ladies' Mile! Let's turn back.

HE. – What's the good? There's a cloud on Elysium Hill, and that means it's foggy all down the Mall. We'll go on. It'll blow away before we get to the Convent, perhaps. Jove! It *is* chilly.

SHE. – You feel it, fresh from below. Put on your ulster. What do you think of my cape?

HE. – Never ask a man his opinion of a woman's dress when he is desperately and abjectly in love with the wearer. Let me look. Like everything else of yours, it's perfect. Where did you get it from?

SHE. – He gave it me, on Wednesday – our wedding day, you know.

HE. – The deuce he did! He's growing generous in his old age. D'you like all that frilly, bunchy stuff at the throat? I don't.

SHE. – Don't you? "Kind Sir, o' your courtesy,
                    As you go by the town, Sir,
                  Pray you o' your love for me,
                    Buy me a russet gown, Sir."

HE. – I won't say: "Keek into the draw-well, Janet, Janet." Only wait a little, darling, and you shall be stocked with russet gowns and everything else.

SHE. – And when the frocks wear out, you'll get me new ones – and everything else?

HE. – Assuredly.

SHE. – I wonder!

HE. – Look here, Sweetheart, I didn't spend two days and two nights in the train to hear you wonder. I thought we'd settled all that at Shaifazehat.

SHE. (*Dreamily*) – At Shaifazehat? Does the Station go on still? That was ages and ages ago. It must be crumbling to pieces. All except the Amirtollah road. I don't believe *that* could crumble till the Day of Judgement.

HE. – You think so? What is the mood now?

SHE. – I can't tell. How cold it is! Let us get on quickly.

HE. – Better walk a little. Stop your men and get out. What's the matter with you this evening, dear?

SHE. – Nothing. You must grow accustomed to my ways. If I'm boring you I can go home. Here's Captain Congleton coming. I dare say he'll be willing to escort me.

HE. – Goose! Between *us*, too! *Damn* Captain Congleton. There!

SHE. – Chivalrous knight. Is it your habit to swear much in talking? It jars a little, and you might swear at me.

HE. – My angel! I didn't know what I was saying, and you changed so quickly that I couldn't follow. I'll apologise in dust and ashes.

SHE. – Spare those. There'll be enough of them later on. (*As the Captain rides by*) Good night, Captain Congleton. Going to the singing quadrilles already? What dances am I giving you next week? No! You must have written them down wrong. Five and Seven, *I* said. If you've made a mistake I certainly don't intend to suffer for it. You must alter your programme.

HE. (*After a pause*) – I thought you told me that you had not been going out much this season?

SHE. – Quite true, but when I do I dance with Captain Congleton. He dances very nicely.

HE. – And sit out with him I suppose?

SHE. – Yes. Have you any objection? Shall I stand under the chandelier in future?

HE. – What does he talk to you about?

SHE. – What do men talk about when they sit out?

HE. – Ugh! Don't! Well now I'm up, you must dispense with the fascinating Congleton for a while. I don't like him.

SHE. (*After a long pause*) – Do you know what you have said?

HE. – Can't say that I do exactly. I'm not in the best of tempers.

SHE. – So I see – and feel. My true and faithful lover, where is your "eternal constancy," "unalterable trust" and "reverent devotion"? I remember those phrases: you seem to have forgotten them. I mention a man's name –

HE. – A good deal more than that.

SHE. – Well, speak to him about a dance – perhaps the last dance that I shall ever dance in my life before I – before I go away; and you at once distrust and insult me.

HE. – I never said a word.

SHE. – How much did you imply? Guy, is *this* amount of confidence to be our stock to start the new life on?

HE. – No, of course not. I didn't mean that. On my word and honour I didn't. Let it pass, dear. Please let it pass.

SHE. – This once – yes – and a second time, and again and again, all through the years when I shall be unable to resent it. You want too much, my Lancelot, and – you know too much.

HE. – How do you mean?

SHE. – That is a part of the punishment. There cannot be perfect trust between us.

HE. – In Heaven's name, why not?

SHE. – Hush! The other Place is quite enough. Ask yourself.

HE. – I don't follow.

SHE. – You trust me so implicitly that when I look at another man – Never mind. Guy, have you ever made love to a girl – a good girl?

HE. – Something of the sort. Centuries ago – in the Dark Ages, before I ever met you, dear.

SHE. – Tell me what you said to her.

HE. – What does a man say to a girl? I've forgotten.

SHE. – *I* remember. He tells her that he trusts her and worships the ground she walks on, and that he'll love and honour and protect her till her dying day; and so she marries in that belief. At least, I speak of one girl who was *not* protected.

HE. – Well, and then?

SHE. – And then, Guy, and then, that girl needs ten times the love and trust and honour – yes, *honour* – that was enough when she was only a mere wife if – if – the second life she elects to lead is to be made even bearable. Do you understand?

HE. – Even bearable! It'll be Paradise.

SHE. – Ah! Can you give me all I've asked for – not now, nor a few months later, but when you begin to think of what you might have done if you had kept your own appointment and your caste here – when you begin to look upon me as a drag and a burden? I shall want it most then, Guy, for there will be no one in the wide world but you.

HE. – You're a little overtired tonight, Sweetheart, and you're taking a stage view of the situation. After the necessary business in the Courts, the road is clear to –

SHE. – "The holy state of matrimony!" Ha! Ha! Ha!

HE. – Ssh! Don't laugh in that horrible way!

SHE. – I – I – c-c-c-can't help it! Isn't it too absurd! Ah! Ha! Ha! Ha! Guy stop me quick or I shall – l-l-laugh till we get to the Church.

HE. – For goodness sake, stop! Don't make an exhibition of yourself. What is the matter with you?

SHE. – N-n-nothing. I'm better now.

HE. – That's all right. One moment, dear. There's a little wisp of hair got loose from behind your right ear and it's straggling over your cheek. So!

SHE. – Thank'oo. I'm 'f'aid my hat's on one side, too.

HE. – What do you wear these huge dagger bonnet-skewers for? They're big enough to kill a man with.

SHE. – Oh! Don't kill *me,* though. You're sticking it into my head! Let me do it. You men are so clumsy.

HE. – Have you had many opportunities of comparing us – in this sort of work?

SHE. – Guy, what is my name?

HE. – Eh? I don't follow.

SHE. – Here's my card case. Can you read?

HE. – Yes. Well?

SHE. – Well, that answers your question. You know the other man's name. Am I sufficiently humbled, or would you like to ask me if there is anyone else?

HE. – I see now. My darling I never meant that for an instant. I was only joking. There! Lucky there's no one on the road. They'd be scandalised.

SHE. – They'll be more scandalised before the end.

HE. – Do-on't! I don't like you to talk in that way.

SHE. – Unreasonable man! Who asked me to face the situation and accept it? Tell me, do I look like Mrs Penner? *Do* I look like a naughty woman? *Swear* I don't? Give me your word of honour, my *honourable* friend, that I'm not like Mrs Buzgago. That's the way she stands, with her hands clasped at the back of her head. D'you like that?

HE. – Don't be affected.

SHE. – I'm not. I'm Mrs Buzgago. Listen!

"Pendant une anne, toute entière
   Le regiment n'a pas r'paru
Au Ministère de la Guerre;
   On le r'porta comme perdu.
On se r'noncait à r'trouver sa trace,
   Quand un matin subitement,
On le vit r'paraître sur la place,
   Le Colonel toujours en avant."

That's the way she rolls her r's. Am I like her?

HE. – No, but I object when you go on like an actress and sing stuff of that kind. Where in the world did you pick up the *Chanson du Colonel*? It isn't a drawing-room song. It isn't proper.

SHE. – Mrs Buzgago taught it me. She is both drawing-room and proper, and in another month she'll shut her drawing-room to me, and thank God she isn't as improper as I am. Oh, Guy, Guy! I wish I was like some women and had no scruples about – what is it? – "wearing a corpse's hair and being false to the bread they eat".

HE. – I am only a man of limited intelligence and, just now, very bewildered. When you have quite finished flashing through all your moods tell me, and I'll try to understand the last one.

SHE. – Moods, Guy! I haven't any. I'm sixteen years old and you're just twenty, and you've been waiting for two hours outside the school in the cold. And now I've met you, and now we're walking home together. Does that suit you, My Imperial Majesty?

HE. – No. We aren't children. Why can't you be rational?

SHE. – He asks me that when I'm going to commit social suicide for his sake, and, and I don't want to be French and rave about *ma mère,* but have I ever told you that I have a mother, and a brother who was my pet before I married? He's married now. Can't you imagine the pleasure that the news of the elopement will give him? Have you any people at home, Guy, to be pleased with your performances?

HE. – One or two. We can't make omelettes without breaking eggs.

SHE. – (*Slowly*) I don't see the necessity –

HE. – Hah! What do you mean?

SHE. – Shall I speak the truth?

HE. – Under the circumstances, perhaps it would be as well.

SHE. – Guy, I'm afraid.

HE. – I thought we'd settled all that. What of?

SHE. – Of you?

HE. – Oh, damn it all! The old business! This is too bad!

SHE. – Of *you*.

HE. – And what now?

SHE. – What do you think of me?

HE. – Beside the question altogether. What do you intend to do?

SHE. – I daren't risk it. I'm afraid. If I could only cheat –

HE. – No, thanks. That's the one point on which I have any notion of Honour. I won't eat His salt and steal too. I'll loot openly or not at all.

SHE. – I never meant anything else.

HE. – Then why in the world do you pretend not to be willing to come?

SHE. – It's *not* pretence, Guy. I am afraid.

HE. – Please explain.

SHE. – It can't last, Guy. It can't last. You'll get angry, and then you'll swear, and then you'll get jealous, and then you'll mistrust me – you do now – and you yourself will be the best reason for doubting. And I – what shall I do? I shall be no better than Mrs Buzgago found out – no better than anyone. And you'll know that. Oh, Guy, can't you *see*?

HE. – I see that you are desperately unreasonable, little woman.

SHE. – There! The moment I begin to object you get angry. What will you do when I am only your property – stolen property? It can't be, Guy. It can't be! I thought it could, but it can't. You'll get tired of me.

HE. – I tell you I shall not. Won't anything make you understand that?

SHE. – There, can't you see? If you speak to me like that now, you'll call me horrible names later, if I don't do everything as you like. And if you were cruel to me, Guy, where should I go – where should I go? I can't trust you. Oh! I *can't* trust you!

HE. – I suppose I ought to say that I *can* trust you. I've ample reason.

SHE. – Please don't, dear. It hurts as much as if you hit me.

HE. – It isn't exactly pleasant for me.

SHE. – I can't help it. I wish I were dead! I can't trust you and I don't trust myself. Oh, Guy, let it die away and be forgotten!

HE. – Too late now. I don't understand you – I won't – and I can't trust myself to talk this evening. May I call tomorrow?

SHE. – Yes. *No!* Oh give me time! The day after. I get into my *'rickshaw* here and meet Him at Peliti's. You ride.

HE. – I'll go on to Peliti's, too. I think I want a drink. My world's knocked about my ears and the stars are falling. Who are those brutes howling in the Old Library?

SHE. – They're rehearsing the singing quadrilles for the Fancy Ball. Can't you hear Mrs Buzgago's voice? She has a solo. It's quite a new idea. Listen!

MRS BUZGAGO. (*in the Old Library, con. molt. exp.*)

> "See saw! Margery Daw!
> Sold her bed to lie upon straw.
> Wasn't she a silly slut
> To sell her bed and lie upon dirt?"

Captain Congleton, I'm going to alter that to "flirt". It sounds better.

HE. – No, I've changed my mind about the drink. Goodnight, little lady. I shall see you tomorrow?

SHE. – Ye-es. Goodnight, Guy. Don't be angry with me.

HE. – Angry! You know I trust you absolutely. Goodnight and – God bless you!

(*Three seconds later. Alone.*) Hmm! I'd give something to discover whether there's another man at the back of all this.

A SECOND-RATE WOMAN

"Est fuga, volvitur rota,
    On we drift: where looms the dim port?
One, Two, Three, Four, Five contribute their quota:
    Something is gained if one caught but the import,
Show it us, Hugues of Saxe-Gotha."
                    – Master Hugues of Saxe-Gotha.

"**D**ressed! Don't tell me that woman ever dressed in her life. She stood in the middle of the room while her *ayah* – no, her husband – it must have been a man – threw her clothes at her. She then did her hair with her fingers, and rubbed her bonnet in the flue under the bed. I know she did, as well as if I had assisted at the orgy. Who is she?" said Mrs Hauksbee.

"Don't!" said Mrs Mallowe feebly. "You make my head ache. I'm miserable today. Stay me with *fondants,* comfort me with chocolates, for I am – Did you bring anything from Peliti's?"

"Questions to begin with. You shall have the sweets when you have answered them. Who and what is the creature? There were at least half-a-dozen men round her, and she appeared to be going to sleep in their midst."

"Delville," said Mrs Mallowe, "'Shady' Delville, to distinguish her from Mrs Jim of that ilk. She dances as untidily as she dresses I believe, and her husband is somewhere in Madras. Go and call, if you are so interested."

"What have I to do with Shigramitish women? She merely caught my attention for a minute, and I wondered at the attraction that a dowd has for a certain type of man. I expected to see her walk out of her clothes – until I looked at her eyes."

"Hooks and eyes, surely," drawled Mrs Mallowe.

"Don't be clever, Polly. You make my head ache. And round this hayrick stood a crowd of men – a positive crowd!"

"Perhaps they also expected – "

"Polly, don't be Rabelaisian!"

Mrs Mallowe curled herself up comfortably on the sofa and turned her attention to the sweets. She and Mrs Hauksbee shared the same house at Simla; and these things befell two seasons after the matter of Otis Yeere which has been already recorded.

Mrs Hauksbee stepped into the verandah and looked down upon the Mall, her forehead puckered with thought.

"Hah!" said Mrs Hauksbee shortly. "Indeed!"

"What is it?" said Mrs Mallowe sleepily.

"That dowd and The Dancing Master – to whom I object."

"Why to The Dancing Master? He is a middle-aged gentleman, of reprobate and romantic tendencies, and tries to be a friend of mine."

"Then make up your mind to lose him. Dowds cling by nature, and I should imagine that this animal – how terrible her bonnet looks from above! – is especially clingsome."

"She is welcome to The Dancing Master so far as I am concerned. I never could take an interest in a monotonous liar. The frustrated aim of his life is to persuade people that he is a bachelor."

"O-oh! I think I've met that sort of thing before. And isn't he?"

"No. He confided that to me a few days ago. Ugh! Some men ought to be killed."

"What happened then?"

"He posed as the horror of horrors – a misunderstood man. Heaven knows the *femme incomprise* is sad enough and bad enough – but the other thing!"

"And so fat too. *I* should have laughed in his face. Men seldom confide in me. How is it they come to you!"

"For the sake of impressing me with their careers in the past. Protect me from men with confidences!"

"And yet you encourage them?"

"What can I do? They talk, I listen; and they vow that I am sympathetic. I know I always profess astonishment even when the plot is – of the most old possible."

"Yes. Men are so unblushingly explicit if they are once allowed to talk, whereas women's confidences are full of reservation and fibs except – "

"When they go mad and babble of the Unutterabilities after a week's acquaintance. Even then, they always paint themselves like Mrs Gummidge – throwing cold water on *him*. Really, if you come to consider, we know a great deal more of men than of our own sex."

"And the extraordinary thing is that men will never believe it. They say we are trying to hide something."

"They are generally doing that on their own account – and very clumsily they hide. Alas! These chocolates pall upon me, and I haven't eaten more than a dozen. I think I shall go to sleep."

"Then you'll get fat, dear. If you took more exercise and a more intelligent interest in your neighbours you would – "

"Be as universally loved as Mrs Hauksbee. You're a darling in many ways and I like you – you are not a woman's woman – but why do you trouble yourself about mere human beings?"

"Because in the absence of angels, who I am sure would be horribly dull, men and women are the most fascinating things in the whole wide world, lazy one. I am interested in The Dowd – I am interested in The Dancing Master – I am interested in the Hawley Boy – and I am interested in you."

"Why couple me with the Hawley Boy? He is your property."

"Yes, and in his own guileless speech, I'm making a good thing out of him. When he is slightly more reformed, and has passed his Higher Standard, or whatever the authorities think fit to exact from him, I shall select a pretty little girl, the Holt Girl I think, and" – here she waved her hands airily – " 'whom Mrs Hauksbee hath joined together let no man put asunder.' That's all."

"And when you have yoked May Holt with the most notorious detrimental in Simla and earned the undying hatred of Mamma Holt, what will you do with me, Dispenser of the Destinies of the Universe?"

Mrs Hauksbee dropped into a low chair in front of the fire, and, chin in hand, gazed long and steadfastly at Mrs Mallowe.

"I do not know," she said, shaking her head, "what I shall do with you, dear. It's obviously impossible to marry you to some-one else – your husband would object, and the experiment might not be successful after all. I think I shall begin by preventing you from – what is it? – 'sleeping on ale-house benches and snoring in the sun'."

"Don't! I don't like your quotations. They are so rude. Go to the Library and bring me new books."

"While you sleep? No! If you don't come with me, I shall spread your newest frock on my *'rickshaw*-bow, and when any one asks me what I am doing, I shall say that I am going to the dressmaker's to get it let out. I shall take care that Mrs MacNamara sees me! Put your things on, there's a good girl."

Mrs Mallowe groaned and obeyed, and the two went off to the Library, where they found Mrs Delville and the man who went by the nickname of The Dancing Master. By that time Mrs Mallowe was awake and eloquent.

"That is the Creature!" said Mrs Hauksbee, with the air of one pointing out a slug in the road.

"No," said Mrs Mallowe, "the man is the Creature. Ugh! Good evening, Mr Bent. I thought you were coming to tea this evening."

"Surely it was for tomorrow, was it not?" answered The Dancing Master. "I understood – I fancied – I'm so sorry – how very unfortunate!"

But Mrs Mallowe had passed on.

"For the practised equivocator you said he was," murmured Mrs Hauksbee, "he strikes me as a failure. Now wherefore should he have preferred a walk with The Dowd to tea with us? Elective affinities, I suppose – both grubby. Polly, I'd never forgive that woman as long as the world rolls."

"I forgive every woman everything," said Mrs Mallowe. "He will be a sufficient punishment for her. What a common voice she has!"

Mrs Delville's voice was not pretty, her carriage was even less lovely, and her raiment was strikingly neglected. All these facts Mrs Mallowe absorbed over the top of a magazine.

"Now, what is there in her?" said Mrs Hauksbee. "Do you see what I meant about the clothes falling off? If I were a man I would perish sooner than be seen with that ragbag. And yet, she has good eyes but – oh!"

"What is it?"

"She doesn't know how to use them! On my honour she does not. Look! Oh, look! Untidiness I can endure, but ignorance never! The woman's a fool."

"Hsh! She'll hear you."

"All the women in Simla are fools. She'll think I mean some-one else. Now she's going out. What a thoroughly objectionable couple she and The Dancing Master make! Which reminds me. Do you suppose they'll ever dance together?"

"Wait and see. I don't envy her the conversation of The Dancing Master – loathly man! His wife ought to be up here before long?"

"Do you know anything about him?"

"Only what he told me. It may be all a fiction. He married a girl bred in the country, I think, and, being an honourable, chivalrous soul, told me that he repented his bargain and sent her to her mother as often as possible – a person who has lived in the Doon since the memory of man and goes to Mussoorie when other people go home. The wife is with her at present. So he says."

"Babies?"

"One only, but he talks of his wife in a revolting way. I hated him for it. He thought he was being epigrammatic and brilliant."

"That is a vice peculiar to men. I dislike him because he is generally in the wake of some girl, to the disgust of the eligibles. He will persecute May Holt no more, unless I am much mistaken."

"No. I think Mrs Delville may occupy his attention for a while."

"Do you suppose she knows that he is the head of a family?"

"Not from his lips. He swore me to eternal secrecy. Wherefore I tell you. Don't you know that type of man?"

"Not intimately, thank goodness! As a general rule when a man begins to abuse his wife to me, I find that the Lord gives me wherewith to answer him according to his folly; and we part with a coolness between us. I laugh."

"I'm different. I've no sense of humour."

"Cultivate it, then. It has been my mainstay for more years than I care to think about. A well-educated sense of humour will save a woman when religion, training and home influences fail. And we may all need salvation sometimes."

"Do you suppose that the Delville woman has humour?"

"Her dress betrays her. How can a thing who wears her *supplément* under her left arm have any notion of the fitness of things – much less their folly. If she discards The Dancing

Master after having once seen him dance, I may respect her. Otherwise – "

"But are we not both assuming a great deal too much, dear? You saw the woman at Peliti's – half an hour later you saw her walking with The Dancing Master – an hour later you meet her here at the Library."

"Still with The Dancing Master, remember."

"Still with The Dancing Master, I admit, but why on the strength of that should you imagine – "

"I imagine nothing. I have no imagination. I am only convinced that The Dancing Master is attracted to The Dowd because he is objectionable in almost every way and she in every other. If I know the man as you have described him, he holds his wife in deadly subjection at present."

"She is twenty years younger than he."

"Poor wretch! And, in the end, after he has posed and swaggered and lied – he has a mouth under that ragged moustache simply made for lies – he will be rewarded according to his merits."

"I wonder what those really are," said Mrs Mallowe.

But Mrs Hauksbee, her face close to the shelf of the new books, was humming softly: "*What shall he have who killed the Deer?*" She was a lady of unfettered speech.

One month later, she announced her intention of calling upon Mrs Delville. Both Mrs Hauksbee and Mrs Mallowe were in morning wrappers and there was a great peace in the land.

"I should go as I was," said Mrs Mallowe. "It would be a delicate compliment to her style."

Mrs Hauksbee studied herself in the glass.

"Assuming for a moment that she ever darkened these doors, I should put on this robe, after all the others, to show her what a morning wrapper ought to be. It might enliven her. As it is, I shall go in the dove-coloured – sweet emblem of youth and innocence – and shall put on my new gloves."

"If you really are going, dirty tan would be too good; and you know that dove-colour spots with the rain."

"I care not. I may make her envious. At least I shall try, though one cannot expect very much from a woman who puts a lace tucker into her habit."

"Heavens! When did she do that?"

"Yesterday – riding with The Dancing Master. I met them at the back of Jakko and the rain had made the lace lie down. To complete the effect, she was wearing an unclean Terai with the elastic under her chin. I felt almost too well content to take the trouble to despise her."

"The Hawley Boy was riding with you. What did he think?"

"Does a boy ever notice these things? Should I like him if he did? He stared in the rudest way, and just when I thought he had seen the elastic, he said: 'There's something very taking about that face.' I rebuked him on the spot. I don't approve of boys being taken by faces."

"Other than your own. I shouldn't be in the least surprised if the Hawley Boy immediately went to call."

"I forbade him. Let her be satisfied with The Dancing Master, and his wife when she comes up. I'm rather curious to see Mrs Bent and the Delville woman together."

Mrs Hauksbee departed and, at the end of an hour, returned slightly flushed.

"There is no limit to the treachery of youth! I ordered the Hawley Boy, as he valued my patronage, not to call. The first person I stumble over – literally stumble over – in her poky, dark, little drawing room is, of course, the Hawley Boy. She kept us waiting ten minutes, and then emerged as though she had been tipped out of the dirty clothes basket. You know my way, dear, when I am at all put out. I was superior, *crrrushingly* superior! Lifted my eyes to Heaven and had heard of nothing – dropped my eyes on the carpet and 'really didn't know' – played with my card case and 'supposed so'. The

Hawley Boy giggled like a girl, and I had to freeze him with scowls between the sentences."

"And she?"

"She sat in a heap on the edge of a couch, and managed to convey the impression that she was suffering from stomach ache, at the very least. It was all I could do not to ask after her symptoms. When I rose, she grunted just like a buffalo in the water – too lazy to move."

"Are you certain – ?"

"Am I blind, Polly? Laziness, sheer laziness, nothing else – or her garments were only constructed for sitting down in. I stayed for a quarter of an hour trying to penetrate the gloom, to guess what her surroundings were like, while she stuck out her tongue."

"Lu-*cy!*"

"Well – I'll withdraw the tongue, though I'm sure if she didn't do it when I was in the room, she did the minute I was outside. At any rate, she lay in a lump and grunted. Ask the Hawley Boy, dear. I believe the grunts were meant for sentences, but she spoke so indistinctly that I can't swear to it."

"You are incorrigible, simply."

"I am not! Treat me civilly, give me peace with honour, don't put the only available seat facing the window, and a child may eat jam in my lap before Church. But I resent being grunted at. Wouldn't you? Do you suppose that she communicates her views on life and love to The Dancing Master in a set of modulated 'Grumphs'?"

"You attach too much importance to The Dancing Master."

"He came as we went, and The Dowd grew almost cordial at the sight of him. He smiled greasily, and moved about that darkened dog kennel in a suspiciously familiar way."

"Don't be uncharitable. Any sin but that I'll forgive."

"Listen to the voice of History. I am only describing what I saw. He entered, the heap on the sofa revived slightly, and the

69

Hawley Boy and I came away together. I felt it my duty to lecture him severely for going there. And that's all."

"Now for Pity's sake leave the wretched creature and The Dancing Master alone. They never did you any harm."

"No harm! To dress as an example and a stumbling block for half Simla, and then to find this Person who is dressed by the hand of God – not that I wish to disparage *Him* for a moment, but you know the cheap milliner way he attires those lilies of the field – this Person draws the eyes of men – and some of them nice men! It's almost enough to make one discard clothing. I told the Hawley Boy so."

"And what did that sweet youth do?"

"Turned shell-pink and looked across the far blue hills like a distressed cherub. Am I talking wildly, Polly? Let me say my say and I shall be calm. Otherwise I may go abroad and disturb Simla with a few original reflections. Excepting always your own sweet self, there isn't a single woman in the land who understands me when I am – what's the word?"

"Insane," suggested Mrs Mallowe.

"Exactly! And now let us have tiffin. The demands of Society are exhausting, and as Mrs Delville says – " Here Mrs Hauksbee, to the horror of the servants, lapsed into a series of grunts, while Mrs Mallowe stared in lazy surprise.

"'God gie us a gude conceit of oorselves,' " said Mrs Hauksbee piously, returning to her natural speech. "Now, in any other woman that would have been vulgar. I am consumed with curiosity to see Mrs Bent. I expect complications."

"Women of one idea," said Mrs Mallowe shortly, "all complications are as old as the hills! I have lived through or near all – *all* – ALL!"

"And yet do not understand that men and women never behave twice alike? I am old who was young – if ever I put my head in your lap, you dear, big sceptic, you will learn that my parting is gauze – but never, no never, have I lost my interest in men and women. Polly, I shall see this business out to the bitter end."

"I am going to sleep," said Mrs Mallowe calmly. "I never interfere with men or women unless I am compelled," and she retired with dignity to her own room.

Mrs Hauksbee's curiosity was not long left ungratified, for Mrs Bent came up to Simla a few days after the conversation faithfully reported above, and pervaded the Mall by her husband's side.

"Behold!" said Mrs Hauksbee, thoughtfully rubbing her nose. "That is the last link of the chain, if we omit the husband of the Delville, whoever he may be. Let me consider. The Bents and the Delvilles inhabit the same hotel; and the Delville is detested by the Waddy – do you know the Waddy? – who is almost as big a dowd. The Waddy also abominates the male Bent, for which, if her other sins do not weigh too heavily, she will eventually be caught up to Heaven."

"Don't be irreverent," said Mrs Mallowe. "I like Mrs Bent's face."

"I am discussing the Waddy," returned Mrs Hauksbee loftily. "The Waddy will take the female Bent apart, after having borrowed – yes! – everything that she can, from hairpins to babies' bottles. Such, my dear, is life in a hotel. The Waddy will tell the female Bent facts and fictions about The Dancing Master and The Dowd."

"Lucy, I should like you better if you were not always looking into people's back bedrooms."

"Anybody can look into their front drawing rooms; and remember whatever I do, and wherever I look, I never talk – as the Waddy will. Let us hope that The Dancing Master's greasy smile and manner of the pedagogue will 'soften the heart of that cow' his wife. If mouths speak truth, I should think that little Mrs Bent could get very angry on occasion."

"But what reason has she for being angry?"

71

"What reason? The Dancing Master in himself is a reason. Remember, 'If in his life some trivial errors fall, look in his face, and you'll believe them all.' I am prepared to credit any evil of The Dancing Master, because I hate him so. And The Dowd is so disgustingly badly dressed – "

"That she, too, is capable of every iniquity? I always prefer to believe the best of everybody. It saves so much trouble."

"Very good. I prefer to believe the worst. It saves useless expenditure of sympathy. And you may be quite certain that the Waddy believes with me."

Mrs Mallowe sighed and made no answer.

The conversation was holden after dinner while Mrs Hauksbee was dressing for a dance.

"I am too tired to go," pleaded Mrs Mallowe, and Mrs Hauksbee left her in peace till two in the morning, when she was aware of emphatic knocking at her door.

"Don't be very angry, dear," said Mrs Hauksbee. "My idiot of an *ayah* has gone home, and, as I hope to sleep tonight, there isn't a soul in the place to unlace me.

"Oh, this is too bad!" said Mrs Mallowe sulkily.

"Can't help it. I'm a lone, lorn grass widow, but I will not sleep in my stays. And such news, too! Oh, *do* unlace me, there's a darling! The Dowd – The Dancing Master – I and the Hawley Boy – you know the North verandah?"

"How can I do anything if you spin round like this?" protested Mrs Mallowe, fumbling with the knot of the lace.

"Oh! I forgot. I must tell my tale without the aid of your eyes. Do you know you've lovely eyes, dear. Well to begin with, I took the Hawley Boy to set out with."

"Did he want much taking?"

"Lots! There was an arrangement of loose boxes in the verandah, and *she* was in the next one talking to *him*."

"Which? How? Explain."

"You know what I mean – The Dowd and The Dancing Master. We could hear every word, and we listened shamelessly – 'specially the Hawley Boy. Polly, I quite love that woman!"

"This is interesting. There! Now turn round. What happened?"

"One moment. Ah-h! Blessed relief. I've been looking forward to taking them off for the last half hour – which is ominous at my time of life. But, as I was saying, we listened and heard The Dowd drawl worse than ever. She drops her final g's like a barmaid or a blue-blooded Aide-de-Camp. 'Look he-ere, you're gettin' too fond o' me,' she said, and The Dancing Master owned that it was so in language that nearly made me ill. The Dowd reflected for a while, then we heard her say: 'Look he-ere, Mister Bent, why are you such an awful liar?' I nearly exploded while The Dancing Master denied the charge. It seems that he never told her he was a married man."

"I said he wouldn't."

"And she had taken this to heart, on personal grounds, I suppose. She drawled along for five minutes, reproaching him with his perfidy, and grew quite motherly. 'Now you've got a nice little wife of your own – you have,' she said. 'She's ten times too good for a fat old man like you, and, look he-ere, you never told me a word about her, and I've been thinkin' about it a good deal, and I think you're a liar.' Wasn't that delicious? The Dancing Master maundered and raved till the Hawley Boy suggested that he should burst in and beat him. His voice runs up into an impassioned squeak when he is afraid. The Dowd must be an extraordinary woman. She explained that, had he been a bachelor, she might not have objected to his devotion, but since he was a married man and the father of a very nice baby, she considered him a hypocrite, and this she repeated twice. She wound up her drawl with: 'An' I'm tellin' you this because your wife is angry with me, an' I hate quarrellin' with any other woman, an' I like your wife. You know how you have behaved for the last six weeks. You shouldn't have done it, indeed you shouldn't. You're too old an' too fat.' Can't you imagine how The Dancing Master would wince at that! 'Now go away,' she said. 'I don't want to tell you what I think of you, because I think you are not nice. I'll stay he-ere till the next dance begins.' Did you think that the creature had so much in her?"

"I never studied her as closely as you did. It sounds unnatural. What happened?"

"The Dancing Master attempted blandishment, reproof, jocularity and the style of the Lord High Warden, and I had almost to pinch the Hawley Boy to make him keep quiet. She grunted at the end of each sentence and, in the end, *he* went away swearing to himself, quite like a man in a novel. He looked more objectionable than ever. I laughed. I love that woman – in spite of her clothes. And now I'm going to bed. What do you think of it?"

"I shan't begin to think till the morning," said Mrs Mallowe, yawning. "Perhaps she spoke the truth. They do fly into it by accident sometimes."

Mrs Hauksbee's account of her eavesdropping was an ornate one, but truthful in the main. For reasons best known to herself, Mrs "Shady" Delville had turned upon Mr Bent and rent him limb from limb, casting him away limp and disconcerted ere she withdrew the light of her eyes from him permanently. Being a man of resource, and anything but pleased in that he had been called both old and fat, he gave Mrs Bent to understand that he had, during her absence in the Doon, been the victim of unceasing persecution at the hands of Mrs Delville, and he told the tale so often and with such eloquence, that he ended in believing it, while his wife marvelled at the manners and customs of some women. When the situation showed signs of languishing, Mrs Waddy was always on hand to wake the smouldering fires of suspicion in Mrs Bent's bosom and to contribute generally to the peace and comfort of the hotel. Mr Bent's life was not a happy one, for if Mrs Waddy's story were true, he was, argued his wife, untrustworthy to the last degree. If his own statement were true, his charms of manner and conversation were so great that he needed constant surveillance. And he received it, till he repented genuinely of his marriage and neglected his personal appearance. Mrs Delville alone in the hotel was unchanged. She removed her chair some six places towards the head of the table, and occasionally in the twilight ventured on timid overtures of friendship to Mrs Bent, which were repulsed.

"She does it for my sake," hinted the virtuous Bent.

"A dangerous and designing woman," purred Mrs Waddy.

Worst of all, every other hotel in Simla was full!

"Polly, are you afraid of diphtheria?"

"Of nothing in the world except smallpox. Diphtheria kills, but it doesn't disfigure. Why do you ask?"

"Because the Bent baby has got it, and the whole hotel is upside down in consequence. The Waddy has set her five young on the rail and fled. The Dancing Master fears for his precious throat, and that miserable little woman, his wife, has no notion of what ought to be done. She wanted to put it into a mustard bath – for croup!"

"Where did you learn all this?"

"Just now, on the Mall. Dr Howlen told me. The Manager of the hotel is abusing the Bents, and the Bents are abusing the Manager. They are a feckless couple."

"Well. What's on your mind?"

"This; and I know it's a grave thing to ask. Would you seriously object to my bringing the child over here, with its mother?"

"On the most strict understanding that we see nothing of The Dancing Master."

"He will be only too glad to stay away. Polly, you're an angel. The woman really is at her wits' end."

"And you know nothing about her, care less, and would hold her up to public scorn if it gave you a minute's amusement. Therefore you risk your life for the sake of her brat. No, Loo, *I'm* not the angel. I shall keep to my rooms and avoid her. But do as you please – only tell me why you do it."

Mrs Hauksbee's eyes softened; she looked out of the window and back into Mrs Mallowe's face.

"I don't know," said Mrs Hauksbee simply.

"You dear!"

"Polly! – And for aught you knew you might have taken my fringe off. Never do that again without warning. Now we'll get the rooms ready. I don't suppose I shall be allowed to circulate in society for a month."

"And I also. Thank goodness, I shall at last get all the sleep I want."

Much to Mrs Bent's surprise she and the baby were brought over to the house almost before she knew where she was. Bent was devoutly and undisguisedly thankful, for he was afraid of the infection and also hoped that a few weeks in the hotel alone with Mrs Delville might lead to some sort of explanation.

Mrs Bent had cast her jealousy to the winds in her fear for her child's life.

"We can give you good milk," said Mrs Hauksbee to her, "and our house is much nearer to the Doctor's than the hotel, and you won't feel as though you were living in a hostile camp. Where is the dear Mrs Waddy? She seemed to be a particular friend of yours."

"They've all left me," said Mrs Bent bitterly. "Mrs Waddy went first. She said I ought to be ashamed of myself for introducing diseases there, and I'm sure it wasn't my fault that little Dora – "

"How nice!" cooed Mrs Hauksbee. "The Waddy is an infectious disease herself – 'more quickly caught than the plague and the taker runs presently mad'. I lived next door to her at the Elysium, three years ago. Now see, you won't give us the least trouble and I've ornamented all the house with sheets soaked in carbolic. It smells comforting, doesn't it? Remember I'm always in call, and my *ayah's* at your service when yours goes to her meals and – and – if you cry I'll *never* forgive you."

Dora Bent occupied her mother's unprofitable attention through the day and the night. The Doctor called thrice in the twenty-four hours, and the house reeked with the smell of the Condy's Fluid, chlorine water, and carbolic acid washes. Mrs Mallowe kept to her own rooms – she considered that she had made sufficient concessions in the cause of humanity – and Mrs Hauksbee was more esteemed by the doctor as a help in the sickroom than the half-distraught mother.

"I know nothing of illness," said Mrs Hauksbee to the Doctor, "only tell me what to do and I'll do it."

"Keep that crazy woman from kissing the child, and let her have as little to do with the nursing as you possibly can," said the Doctor; "I'd turn her out of the sickroom, but that I honestly believe she'd die of anxiety. She is less than no good, and I depend on you and the *ayahs*, remember."

Mrs Hauksbee accepted the responsibility, even though it painted olive hollows under her eyes and forced her into her oldest dresses. Mrs Bent clung to her with more than childlike faith.

"I know you'll make Dora well, won't you?" she said at least twenty times a day; and twenty times a day Mrs Hauksbee answered valiantly: "Of course I will."

But Dora did not improve, and the Doctor seemed to be always in the house.

"There's some danger of the thing taking a bad turn," he said, "I'll come over between three and four in the morning tomorrow."

"Good gracious!" said Mrs Hauksbee, "He never told me what the turn would be! My education has been horribly neglected; and I have only this foolish mother-woman to fall back upon."

The night wore through slowly, and Mrs Hauksbee dozed in a chair by the fire. There was a dance at Viceregal Lodge, and she dreamed of it till she was aware of Mrs Bent's anxious eyes staring into her own.

"Wake up! Wake up! Do something!" cried Mrs Bent piteously. "Dora's choking to death! Do you mean to let her die?"

Mrs Hauksbee jumped to her feet and bent over the bed. The child was fighting for breath, while the mother wrung her hands in despair.

"Oh, what can I do! What can you do! She won't stay still! I can't hold her. Why didn't the doctor say this was coming?" screamed Mrs Bent. "Won't you help me? She's dying!"

"I – I've never seen a child die before!" stammered Mrs Hauksbee feebly, and then – let no one blame her weakness after the strain of long watching – she broke down, and covered her face with her hands. The *ayahs* on the threshold snored peacefully.

There was a rattle of 'rickshaw wheels below, the clash of an opening door, a heavy step on the stairs, and Mrs Delville entered to find Mrs Bent running round the room and screaming for the Doctor. Mrs Hauksbee, her hands to her ears, and her face buried in the chintz of a chair, was quivering with pain at each cry from the bed and murmuring: "Thank God I never bore a child! O thank God I never bore a child!"

Mrs Delville looked at the bed for an instant, took Mrs Bent by the shoulders and said quietly: "Get me some caustic. Be quick."

The mother obeyed mechanically. Mrs Delville had thrown herself down by the side of the child and was opening its mouth.

"Oh, you're killing her!" cried Mrs Bent. "Where's the Doctor? Leave her alone!"

Mrs Delville made no reply for a minute but busied herself with the child.

"Now the caustic, and hold a lamp behind my left shoulder. Will you do as you are told? The acid bottle, if you don't know what I mean," she said.

A second time Mrs Delville bent over the child. Mrs Hauksbee, her face still hidden, sobbed and shivered. One of the *ayahs* staggered sleepily into the room yawning: "The Doctor has come."

Mrs Delville turned her head:

"You're only just in time," she said. "It was chokin' her when I came an' I've burnt it."

"There was no sign of the membrane getting to the air passages after the last steaming. It was the general weakness, I feared," said the Doctor half to himself, and he whispered as he looked: "You've done what I should have been afraid to do without consultation."

"She was dyin'," said Mrs Delville, under her breath. "Can you do anythin'? What a mercy it was I went to the dance!"

Mrs Hauksbee raised her head.

"Is it all over?" she gasped. "I'm useless. I'm worse than useless! What are *you* doing here?"

She stared at Mrs Delville, and Mrs Bent, realising for the first time who was the Goddess from the machine, stared also.

Then Mrs Delville made explanation, putting on a dirty long glove and smoothing a crumpled and ill-fitting ball dress.

"I was at the dance an' the Doctor was tellin' me about your baby bein' so ill. So I came away early, an' your door was open an' I – I – lost my boy this way six months ago, an' I've been tryin' to forget it ever since, an' I – I – I am very sorry for intrudin' an' anythin' that has happened." Mrs Bent was putting out the Doctor's eye with a lamp as he stooped over Dora.

"Take it away," said the Doctor. "I think the child will do, thanks to you, Mrs Delville. I should have come too late, but, I assure you," – he was addressing himself to Mrs Delville – "I had not the faintest reason to expect this. The membrane must have grown like a mushroom. Will one of you ladies help me, please?"

He had reason for his concluding sentence. Mrs Hauksbee had thrown herself into Mrs Delville's arms, where she was weeping copiously, and Mrs Bent was unpicturesquely mixed up with both, while from the triple tangle came the sound of many sobs and much promiscuous kissing.

"Good gracious! I've spoilt all your beautiful roses!" said Mrs Hauksbee, lifting her head from the lump of crushed gum and calico atrocities on Mrs Delville's shoulder and hurrying to the Doctor.

Mrs Delville picked up her shawl, and slouched out of the room, mopping her eyes with the glove that she had not put on.

"I always said she was more than a woman," sobbed Mrs Hauksbee hysterically, "and *that* proves it!"

Six weeks later, Mrs Bent and Dora had returned to the hotel. Mrs Hauksbee had come out of the Valley of Humiliation, had ceased to reproach herself for her collapse in an hour of bitter need, and was even beginning to direct the affairs of the world as before.

"So nobody died, and everything went off as it should, and I kissed The Dowd, Polly. I feel so old. Does it show in my face?"

"Kisses don't as a rule, do they? Of course you know what the result of The Dowd's providential arrival has been."

"They ought to build her a statue – only no sculptor dare reproduce those skirts."

"Ah!" said Mrs Mallowe quietly. "She has found another reward. The Dancing Master has been smirking through Simla giving every one to understand that she came because of her undying love for him – for him – to save his child, and all Simla naturally believes this."

"But Mrs Bent – "

"Mrs Bent believes it more than anyone else. She won't speak to The Dowd now. Isn't The Dancing Master an angel?"

Mrs Hauksbee lifted up her voice and raged till bedtime. The doors of the two rooms stood open.

"Polly," said a voice from the darkness, "what did that American-heiress-globetrotter girl say last season when she was tipped out of her 'rickshaw turning a corner? Some absurd adjective that made the man who picked her up explode."

" 'Paltry,' " said Mrs Mallowe. "Through her nose – like this – 'Ha-ow pahltry!' "

"Exactly," said the voice. "Ha-ow pahltry it all is!"

"Which?"

"Everything. Babies, Diphtheria, Mrs Bent and The Dancing Master, I whooping in a chair, and The Dowd dropping in from the clouds. I wonder what the motive was – all the motives."

"Um!"

"What do you think?"

"Don't ask me. She was a woman. Go to sleep."

ONLY A SUBALTERN

> "...Not only to enforce by command but to encourage
> by example the energetic discharge of duty and the
> steady endurance of the difficulties and privations
> inseparable from Military Service."
>
> — *Bengal Army Regulations.*

They made Bobby Wick pass an examination at Sandhurst. He was a gentleman before he was gazetted, so, when the Empress announced that "Gentleman-Cadet Robert Hanna Wick" was posted as Second Lieutenant to the Tyneside Tail Twisters at Krab Bokhar, he became an officer and a gentleman, which is an enviable thing; and there was joy in the house of Wick, where Mamma Wick and all the little Wicks fell upon their knees and offered incense to Bobby by virtue of his achievements.

Papa Wick had been a Commissioner in his day, holding authority over three millions of men in the Chota-Buldana Division, building great works for the good of the land, and doing his best to make two blades of grass grow where there was but one before. Of course, nobody knew anything about this in the little English village where he was just "old Mr Wick," and had forgotten that he was a CSI.

He patted Bobby on the shoulder and said: "Well done, my boy!"

There followed, while the uniform was being prepared, an interval of pure delight, during which Bobby took brevet rank as a "man" at the women-swamped tennis parties and tea fights of the village, and, I dare say, had his joining time been extended, would have fallen in love with several girls at once. Little country villages at home are very full of nice girls, because all the young men come out here to make their fortunes.

"India," said Papa Wick, "is the place. I've had thirty years of it and, begad, I'd like to go back again. When you join the Tail Twisters you'll be among friends, if every one hasn't forgotten Wick of Chota-Buldana, and a lot of people will be kind to you for our sakes. The Mother will tell you more about the outfit than I can; but remember this. Stick to your Regiment, Bobby – stick to your Regiment. You'll see men all round you going into the Staff Corps, and doing every possible sort of duty but regimental, and you may be tempted to follow suit. Now, so long as you keep within your allowance, and I haven't stinted you there, stick to the Line – the whole Line and nothing but the Line. Be careful how you back another young fool's bill and you fall in love with a woman twenty years older than yourself, don't tell me about it, that's all."

With these counsels, and many others equally valuable, did Papa Wick fortify Bobby ere that last awful night at Portsmouth when the Officers' Quarters held more inmates than were provided for by the Regulations, and the liberty men of the ships fell foul of the drafts for India, and the battle raged long and loud from the Dockyard Gates even to the slums of Longport, while the drabs of Fratton came down and scratched the faces of the Queen's Officers.

Bobby Wick, with an ugly bruise on his freckled nose, a sick and shaky detachment to manoeuvre in-ship, and the comfort of fifty scornful females to attend to, had no time to feel homesick till the *Malabar* reached mid-Channel, when he combined his emotions with a little guard-visiting and a great deal of nausea.

The Tail Twisters were a most particular Regiment. Those who knew them least said that they were eaten up with "side" . But their reserve and their internal arrangements generally were merely protective diplomacy. Some five years before, the Colonel commanding had looked into the fourteen fearless eyes of seven plump and juicy subalterns who had all applied to enter the Staff Corps, and had asked them why the three stars should he, a Colonel of the Line, command a dashed nursery for double-dashed bottle-suckers who put on condemned tin spurs and rode qualified mokes at the hiatused heads of forsaken Black Regiments. He was a rude man and a terrible. Wherefore the remnant took measures (with the half-butt as an engine of public opinion) till the rumour went abroad that young men who used the Tail Twisters as a crutch to the Staff Corps, had many and varied trials to endure. However, a Regiment has just as much right to its own secrets as a woman.

When Bobby came up from Deolali and took his place among the Tail Twisters, it was gently but firmly borne in upon him that the Regiment was his father and his mother, and his indissolubly wedded wife, and that there was no crime under the canopy of Heaven blacker than that of bringing shame on the Regiment, which was the best-shooting, best-drilled, best set-up, bravest, most illustrious and in all respects most desirable Regiment within the compass of the Seven Seas. He was taught the legends of the Mess Plate, from the great grinning Golden Gods that had come out of the Summer Palace in Pekin to the silver-mounted markhor-horn snuff-mull presented by the last CO (he who spake to the seven subalterns). And every one of those legends told him of battles fought at long odds, without fear as without support; of hospitality catholic as an Arab's; of friendships deep as the sea and steady as the fighting line; of Honours won by hard roads for Honour's sake; and of instant and unquestioning devotion to the Regiment – the Regiment that claims the lives of all and lives for ever.

More than once, too, he came officially into contact with the Regimental Colours which looked like the lining of a bricklayer's hat on the end of a chewed stick. Bobby did not kneel and worship them, because British subalterns are not constructed in that manner. Indeed, he condemned them for their weight at the very moment that they were filling him with awe and other more noble sentiments.

But best of all was the occasion when he moved with the Tail Twisters in review order at the breaking of a November day. Allowing for duty-men and sick, the Regiment was one thousand and eighty strong, and Bobby belonged to them; for was he not a subaltern of the Line – the whole Line and nothing but the Line – as the tramp of two thousand one hundred and sixty sturdy ammunition boots attested? He would not have changed places with Deighton of the Horse Battery, whirling by in a pillar of cloud to a chorus of "Strong right! Strong left!" or Hogan-Yale of the White Hussars, leading his squadron for all it was worth with the price of horseshoes thrown in; or "Tick" Boileau, trying to live up to his fierce blue and gold turban, while the wasps of the Bengal Cavalry stretched to a gallop in the wake of the long, lolloping Walers of the White Hussars.

They fought through the clear cool day, and Bobby felt a little thrill run down his spine when he heard the *tinkle-tinkle-tinkle* of the empty cartridge cases hopping from the breech-blocks after the roar of the volleys; for he knew that he should live to hear that sound in action. The review ended in a glorious chase across the open. Batteries thundering after Cavalry to the huge disgust of the White Hussars, and the Tyneside Tail Twisters hunting a Sikh Regiment, till the lean, lathy Sikhs panted with exhaustion. Bobby was dusty and dripping long before noon, but his enthusiasm was merely focussed – not diminished.

He returned to sit at the feet of Revere, his "skipper," that is to say, the Captain of his Company, and to be instructed in the dark art and mystery of managing men, which is a very large part of the Profession of Arms.

"If you haven't a gift that way," said Revere between puffs of his cheroot, "you'll never be able to get the hang of it, but remember, Bobby, 't isn't the best drill, though drill is nearly everything that howks a Regiment through Hell and out on the other side. It's the man who knows how to handle men – goat-men, swine-men, dog-men, and so on."

"Dormer, for instance," said Bobby, "I think he comes under the head of fool-men. He mopes like a sick owl."

"That's where you make your mistake, my son. Dormer isn't a fool yet, but he's a dashed, dirty soldier, and his Room Corporal makes fun of his socks before kit inspection. Dormer, being two-thirds pure brute, goes into a corner and growls."

"How do you know?" said Bobby, admiringly.

"Because a Company commander has to know these things; because, if he does not know, he may have crime – ay, murder – brewing under his very nose, and yet not see that it's there. Dormer is being badgered out of his mind big as he is – and he hasn't intellect enough to resent it. He's taken to quiet boozing. Bobby, when the butt of a room goes on the drink, or takes to moping by himself, measures are necessary to yank him out of himself."

"What measures? Man can't run round coddling his men forever."

"No. The man would precious soon show him that he was not wanted. You've got to – "

Here the Colour Sergeant entered with some papers. Bobby reflected for a while as Revere looked through the Company forms.

"Does Dormer do anything, Sergeant?" Bobby asked, with the air of one continuing an interrupted conversation.

"No, Sir. Does 'is dooty like a hortomato," said the Sergeant, who delighted in long words. "A dirty soldier, and 'e's under full stoppages for new kit. It's covered with scales, Sir."

"Scales? What scales?"

"Fish scales, Sir. 'E's always pokin' in the mud by the river, an' a-cleanin' them *muchly* fish with 'is thumbs." Revere was still absorbed in the Company papers, and the Sergeant, who was grimly fond of Bobby, continued: "'E generally goes down there when 'e's got 'is skinful, beggin' your pardon, Sir, an' they do say that the more lush – in*heb*riated 'e is, the more fish 'e catches. They call 'im the Looney Fishmonger in the Comp'ny, Sir."

Revere signed the last paper, and the Sergeant retreated.

"It's a filthy amusement," sighed Bobby to himself. Then aloud to Revere: "Are you really worried about Dormer?"

"A little. You see he's never mad enough to send to hospital, or drunk enough to run in, but at any minute he may flare up, brooding and sulking as he does. He resents any interest being shown in him, and the only time I took him out shooting, he all but shot *me* by accident."

"I fish," said Bobby, with a wry face. "I hire a country boat and go down the river from Thursday to Sunday, and the amiable Dormer goes with me – if you can spare us both."

"You blazing young fool!" said Revere, but his heart was full of much more pleasant words.

Bobby, the captain of a country boat, with Private Dormer for mate, dropped down the river on Thursday morning – the Private at the bow, the Subaltern at the helm. The Private glared uneasily at the Subaltern who respected the reserve of the Private.

After six hours, Dormer paced to the stern, saluted, and said: "Beg y' pardon, Sir, but was you ever on the Durh'm Canal?"

"No," said Bobby Wick. "Come and have some tiffin."

They ate in silence. As the evening fell, Private Dormer broke forth, speaking to himself:

"Hi was on the Durh'm Canal, jes' such a night, come next week twelve month, a trailin' of my toes in the water." He smoked and said no more till bedtime.

The witchery of the dawn turned the grey river reaches to purple, gold, and opal: and it was as though the lumbering barge crept across the splendours of a new Heaven.

Private Dormer popped his head out of his blanket and gazed at the glory below and around.

"Well – damn – my – eyes!" said Private Dormer, in an awed whisper. "This 'ere is like a bloomin' gallantry show!" For the rest of the day he was dumb, but achieved an ensanguined filthiness through the cleaning of big fish.

The boat returned on Saturday evening. Dormer had been struggling with speech since noon. As the lines and luggage were being disembarked, he found tongue.

"Beg y' pardon, Sir," he said, "but would you – would you min' shakin' 'ands with me, Sir?"

"Of course not," said Bobby, and he shook accordingly. Dormer returned to barracks and Bobby to Mess.

"He wanted a little quiet and some fishing, I think," said Bobby. "My aunt, but he's a filthy sort of animal! Have you ever seen him clean them *muchly* fish with 'is thumbs?"

"Anyhow," said Revere three weeks later, "he's doing his best to keep his things clean."

When the Spring died, Bobby joined in the general scramble for Hill leave, and to his surprise and delight secured three months.

"As good a boy as I want," said Revere, the admiring skipper.

"The best of the batch," said the Adjutant to the Colonel. "Keep back that young skrimshanker Porkiss, Sir, and let Revere make him sit up."

89

So Bobby departed joyously to Simla Pahar with a tin box of gorgeous raiment.

"Son of Wick – old Wick of Chota-Buldana? Ask him to dinner, dear," said the aged men.

"What a nice boy!" said the matrons and the maids.

"First-class place, Simla. Oh, ri-ipping!" said Bobby Wick and ordered new cord breeches on the strength of it.

"We're in a bad way," wrote Revere to Bobby at the end of two months. "Since you left, the Regiment has taken to fever and is fairly rotten with it – two hundred in hospital, about a hundred in cells – drinking to keep off fever – and the Companies on parade fifteen file strong at the outside. There's rather more sickness in the out-villages than I care for, but then I'm so blistered with prickly heat that I'm ready to hang myself. What's the yarn about your mashing a Miss Haverley up there? Not serious I hope? You're over-young to hang millstones round your neck, and the Colonel will turf you out of that in double quick time if you attempt it."

It was not the Colonel that brought Bobby out of Simla, but a much more to be respected Commandant. The sickness in the out-villages spread, the Bazar was put out of bounds, and then came the news that the Tail Twisters must go into camp. The message flashed to the Hill station: "Cholera – Leave stopped – Officers recalled." Alas, for the white gloves in the neatly soldered boxes, the rides and the dances and picnics that were to be, the love half-spoken and the debt unpaid? Without demur and without question, fast as tonga could fly or pony gallop, back to their Regiments and their Batteries, as though they were hastening to their weddings, fled the subalterns.

Bobby received his mandate on returning from a dance at Viceregal Lodge where he had – but only the Haverley Girl knows what Bobby had said or how many waltzes he had claimed for the next ball. Six in the morning saw Bobby at the tonga office in the drenching rain, the whirl of the last waltz still in his ears, and an intoxication due neither to wine nor waltzing in his brain.

"Good man!" shouted Deighton of the Horse Battery through the mists. "Whar you raise dat tonga? I'm coming with you. Ow! But I've a head and half. *I* didn't sit out all night. They say the Battery's awful bad," and he hummed dolorously:

> "Leave the what at what's-its-name,
> Leave the flock without shelter,
> Leave the corpse uninterred,
> Leave the bride at the altar!"

"My faith! It'll be more bally corpse than bride, though, this journey. Jump in, Bobby!"

On the Umballa platform waited a detachment of officers discussing the latest news from the stricken cantonment, and it was here that Bobby learned the real condition of the Tail Twisters.

"They went into camp," said an elderly Major recalled from the whist tables at Mussoorie to a sickly Native Regiment, "they went into camp with two hundred and ten sick in carts. Two hundred and ten fever cases only, and the balance looking like so many ghosts with sore eyes. A Madras Regiment could have walked through 'em."

"But they were as fit as be-damned when I left them!" said Bobby.

"Then you'd better make them as fit as be-damned when you rejoin," said the Major brutally.

Bobby pressed his forehead against the rain-splashed window pane as the train lumbered across the sodden Doab, and prayed for the health of the Tyneside Tail Twisters.

Naini Tal had sent down her contingent with all speed; the lathering ponies of the Dalhousie Road staggered into Pathankot taxed to the full stretch of their strength; while from cloudy Darjiling the Calcutta Mail whirled up the last straggler of the little army that was to fight a fight, in which was neither medal nor honour for the winning, against an enemy none other than "the sickness that destroyeth in the noon-day".

And as each man reported himself, he said: "This is a bad business," and went about his own forthwith, for every Regiment and Battery in the cantonment was under canvas, the sickness bearing them company.

Bobby fought his way through the rain to the Tail Twisters' temporary Mess, and Revere could have fallen on the boy's neck for the joy of seeing that ugly, wholesome phiz once more.

"Keep 'em amused and interested," said Revere. "They went on the drink, poor fools, after the first two cases, and there was no improvement. Oh, it's good to have you back, Bobby! Porkiss is a – never mind."

Deighton came over from the Artillery camp to attend a dreary Mess dinner, and contributed to the general gloom by nearly weeping over the condition of his beloved Battery. Porkiss so far forgot himself as to insinuate that the presence of the officers could do no earthly good, and that the best thing would be to send the entire Regiment into hospital and let the Doctors look after them. Porkiss was demoralised with fear, nor was his peace of mind restored when Revere said coldly:

"Oh! The sooner you go out the better, if that's your way of thinking. Any public school could send us fifty good men in your place, but it takes time, time, Porkiss, and money and a certain amount of trouble to make a Regiment. S'pose you're the person we go into camp for, eh?"

Whereupon Porkiss was overtaken with a great and chilly fear which a drenching in the rain did not allay, and two days later, quitted this world for another, where, men do fondly hope, allowances are made for the weaknesses of the flesh. The Regimental Sergeant Major looked wearily across the Sergeants' Mess tent when the news was announced.

"There goes the worst of them," he said. "It'll take the best and then, please God, it'll stop."

The Sergeants were silent till one said: "It couldn't be *him!*" and all knew of whom Travis was thinking.

Bobby Wick stormed through the tents of his Company, rallying, rebuking, mildly, as is consistent with the Regulations, chaffing the faint-hearted; hailing the sound into the watery sunlight when there was a break in the weather and bidding them be of good cheer for their trouble was nearly at an end; scuttling on his dun pony round the outskirts of the camp and heading back men, who, with the innate perversity of British soldiers, were always wandering into infected villages, or drinking deeply from rain-flooded pools; comforting the panic-stricken with rude speech, and more than once tending the dying who had no friends – the men without "townies"; organising, with banjoes and burnt cork, Sing-songs which should allow the talent of the Regiment full play; and, generally, as he explained, "playing the giddy garden goat all round".

"You're worth half-a-dozen of us, Bobby," said his skipper in a moment of enthusiasm. "How the devil do you keep it up?"

Bobby made no answer, but had Revere looked into the breast pocket of his coat he might have seen there a sheaf of badly written letters which perhaps accounted for the power that possessed the boy. A letter came to Bobby every other day. The spelling was not above reproach, but the sentiments must have been most satisfactory, for on receipt Bobby's eyes softened marvellously, and he was used to fall into a tender abstraction for a while, ere, shaking his cropped head, he charged into his work anew.

By what power he drew after him the hearts of the roughest, and the Tail Twisters counted in their ranks some rough diamonds indeed, was a mystery to both skipper and CO, who learned from the regimental chaplain that Bobby was considerably more in request in the hospital tents than the Reverend John Emery.

"The men seem fond of you. Are you in the hospitals much?" said the Colonel, who did his daily round and ordered the men to get well with a grimness that did not cover his better grief.

"A little, Sir," said Bobby.

"Shouldn't go there too often if I were you. They say it's not contagious, but there's no use in running unnecessary risks. We can't afford to have you down, y'know."

Six days later, it was with the utmost difficulty that the post runner plashed his way out to the Camp with the Mailbags, for the rain was falling in torrents. Bobby received a letter, bore it off to his tent and, the programme for the next week's Sing-song being satisfactorily disposed of, sat down to answer it. For an hour the unhandy pen toiled over the paper, and where sentiment rose to more than normal tide level Bobby Wick stuck out his tongue and breathed heavily. He was not used to letter-writing.

"Beg y' pardon Sir," said a voice at the tent door; "but Dormer's 'orrid bad, Sir, and they've taken him orf, Sir."

"Damn Private Dormer and you too!" said Bobby Wick, running the blotter over the half-finished letter. "Tell him I'll come in the morning."

" 'E's awful bad, Sir," said the voice hesitatingly. There was an undecided squelching of heavy boots.

"Well?" said Bobby impatiently.

"Excusin' 'imself before and for takin' the liberty, 'e says it would be a comfort for to assist 'im, Sir, if – "

"Bring my pony! Here, come in out of the rain till I'm ready. What blasted nuisances you are! That's brandy. Drink some. You want it. Hang on to my stirrup and tell me if I go too fast."

Strengthened by a four-finger nip which he absorbed without a wink, the Hospital Orderly kept up with the slipping, mud-stained and very disgusted pony as it shambled to the hospital tent.

Private Dormer was certainly "'orrid bad". He had all but reached the stage of collapse and was not pleasant to see.

"What's this, Dormer?" said Bobby bending over the man. "You're not going out this time. You've got to come fishing with me once or twice more yet."

The blue lips parted and in the ghost of a whisper said – "Beg y' pardon, Sir, disturbin' of you now, but would you min' 'oldin' my 'and, Sir?"

Bobby sat on the side of the bed, and the icy cold hand closed on his own like a vice, forcing a lady's ring which was on the little finger deep into the flesh. Bobby set his lips and waited, the water dripping from the hem of his trousers. An hour passed and the grasp of the hand did not relax, nor did the expression of the drawn face change. Bobby with infinite craft lit himself a cheroot with the left hand, his right arm was numbed to the elbow, and resigned himself to a night of pain.

Dawn showed a very white-faced Subaltern sitting on the side of a sick man's cot, and a Doctor in the doorway using language unfit for publication.

"Have you been here all night, you young ass?" said the Doctor.

"There or thereabouts," said Bobby ruefully. "He's frozen on to me."

Dormer's mouth shut with a click. He turned his head and sighed. The clinging hand opened and Bobby's arm fell useless at his side.

"He'll do," said the Doctor quietly. "It must have been a toss-up all through the night. Think you're to be congratulated on this case."

"Oh, bosh!" said Bobby. "I thought the man had gone out long ago – only – only I didn't care to take my hand away. Rub my arm down, there's a good chap. What a grip the brute has!

I'm chilled to the marrow!" He passed out of the tent shivering.

Private Dormer was allowed to celebrate his repulse of Death by strong waters. Four days later, he sat on the side of his cot and said to the patients mildly: "I'd 'a liken to 'a spoken to 'im – so I should."

But at that time Bobby was reading yet another letter – he had the most persistent correspondent of any man in Camp – and was even then about to write that the sickness had abated and in another week at the outside would be gone. He did not intend to say that the chill of a sick man's hand seemed to have struck into the heart whose capacities for affection he dwelt upon at such a length. He did intend to enclose the illustrated programme of the forthcoming Sing-song whereof he was not a little proud. He also intended to write on many other matters which do not concern us, and doubtless would have done so but for the slight feverish headache which made him dull and unresponsive at Mess.

"You are overdoing it, Bobby," said his skipper. "Might give the rest of us the credit of doing a little work. You go on as if you were the whole Mess rolled into one. Take it easy."

"I will," said Bobby. "I'm feeling done up, somehow." Revere looked at him anxiously and said nothing.

There was a flickering of lanterns about the Camp that night, and a rumour that brought men out of their cots to the tent doors, a paddling of the naked feet of doolie-bearers and the rush of a galloping horse.

"Wot's up?" asked twenty tents; and through twenty tents ran the answer – "Wick, 'e's down."

They brought the news to Revere and he groaned. "Anyone but Bobby and I shouldn't have cared! The Sergeant Major was right."

"Not going out this journey," gasped Bobby as he was lifted from the doolie. "Not going out this journey." Then with an air of supreme conviction: "I *can't*, you see."

"Not if I can do anything!" said the Surgeon Major, who had hastened over from the Mess where he had been dining.

He and the regimental Surgeon fought together with Death for the life of Bobby Wick. Their ministrations were interrupted by a hairy apparition in a blue-grey dressing gown who stared in round-eyed horror at the bed and cried: "Ow my Gawd! It can't be *'im!*" until an indignant Hospital Orderly whisked him away.

If care of man and desire to live could have done aught, Bobby would have been saved. As it was, he made a fight of three days, and the Surgeon Major's brow uncreased. "We'll save him yet," he said; and the Surgeon, who though he ranked with a Captain, had a very youthful heart, went out upon the word and pranced joyously in the mud.

"Not going out this journey," whispered Bobby Wick gallantly, at the end of the third day.

"Bravo!" said the Surgeon Major. "That's the way to look at it, Bobby."

As evening fell, a grey shade gathered round Bobby's mouth, and he turned his face to the tent wall wearily. The Surgeon Major frowned.

"I'm awfully tired," said Bobby, very faintly. "What's the use of bothering me with medicine? I – don't – want – it. Let me alone."

The desire for life had departed and Bobby was content to drift away on the easy tide of Death.

"It's no good," said the Surgeon Major. "He doesn't want to live. He's meeting it, poor child." And he blew his nose.

Half a mile away, the regimental band was playing the overture to the Sing-song, for the men had been told that Bobby was out of danger. The clash of the brass and the wail of the horns reached Bobby's ears.

> "Is there a single joy or pain,
> That I should never kno-ow?

You do not love me, 'tis in vain,
Bid me goodbye and go!"

An expression of hopeless irritation crossed the boy's face, and he tried to shake his head.

The Surgeon Major bent down: "What is it, Bobby?"

"Not that waltz," muttered Bobby. "That's our own – our very ownest own – Mummy dear."

With this oracular sentence he sank into the stupor that gave place to death early next morning.

Revere, his eyes red at the rims and his nose very white, went into Bobby's tent to write a letter to Papa Wick which should bow the white head of the ex-Commissioner of Chota-Buldana in the keenest sorrow of his life. Bobby's little store of papers lay in confusion on the table and among them a half-finished letter. The last sentence ran: "So you see, darling, there is really no fear, because as long as I know you care for me and I care for you, nothing can touch me."

Revere stayed in the tent for an hour. When he came out, his eyes were redder than ever.

Private Conklin sat on a turned-down bucket and listened to a not unfamiliar tune. Private Conklin was a convalescent and should have been tenderly treated.

"Ho!" said Private Conklin. "There's another bloomin' orf'cer da-ed."

The bucket shot from under him and his eyes filled with a smithyful of sparks. A tall man in a blue-grey bedgown was regarding him with deep disfavour.

"You ought to take shame for yourself, Conky! Orf'cer? – Bloomin' orf'cer? I'll learn you to misname the likes of 'im. Hangel! *Bloomin'* Hangel! That's wot 'e is!"

And the Hospital Orderly was so satisfied with the justice of the punishment that he did not even order Private Dormer back to his cot.

Rudyard Kipling

Captains Courageous

Harvey Cheyne is the spoilt, precocious son of an over-indulgent millionaire. On an ocean voyage off the Newfoundland coast, he falls overboard and is rescued by a Portuguese fisherman. Never in need of anything in his entire life, it comes as rather a shock to Harvey to be forced to join the crew of the fishing schooner and work there for an entire summer.

By being thrown into an entirely alien world, Harvey has echoes of Kipling's more famous Mowgli from *The Jungle Book*, and, like Mowgli, Harvey learns to adapt and make something of himself. *Captains Courageous* captures with brilliant detail all the colour of the fishing world and reveals it as a convincing model for society as a whole.

The Jungle Book

The Jungle Book is one of the best-loved stories of all time. In Mowgli, the boy who is raised by wolves in the jungle, we see an enduring creation that has gained near-mythical status. And with such unforgettable companions as Father and Mother Wolf, Shere Khan and Bagheera, Mowgli's life and adventures have come to be recognised as a complex fable of mankind. With a rich and vibrant imagination behind layer upon layer of meaning, Kipling has created a pure masterpiece to thrill and delight adult and child alike.

RUDYARD KIPLING

MANY INVENTIONS

Lo, this only have I found, that God hath made man upright; but they have sought out many inventions – Ecclesiastes vii v. 29

Here Kipling adds to the world's catalogue of inventions since the dawn of time with a few of his own notable examples. *Many Inventions* brings together a number of Kipling's short stories and includes such works as 'His Private Honour', 'Brugglesmith' and 'The Record Of Badalia Herodsfoot'. Embracing his eternal preoccupations of Anglo-Indian relations and human sufferings, this collection is a fine example of Kipling's entire work.

THE PHANTOM RICKSHAW
AND OTHER EERIE TALES

The Phantom Rickshaw and Other Eerie Tales brings together four of Kipling's most-loved short stories. Each deals with events that can't quite be explained away, whether a traditional ghost story, a terrifyingly realistic nightmare or a sumptuous and lavish romance. Powerful, exotic and extravagant, these tales are rated, by some, to be the best stories Kipling ever wrote, with 'The Man Who Would Be King' being hailed as the finest story in the English language.

Rudyard Kipling

Plain Tales from the Hills

Plain Tales from the Hills is an outstanding collection of stories of colonial life capturing all the richness of India's sights, sounds and smells. The tales Kipling tells are ones of loss, suffering and broken faith, a far cry from the celebratory patriotism that surrounded the Empire at the time. He writes with haunting passion about the cultural, racial and sexual barriers of the day and the stories resound with a tender, yet tragic, poignancy.

Rewards and Fairies

Rewards and Fairies is a delightful selection of stories and poems from the creator of *The Jungle Book*. Tales of witches, looking-glasses and square toes come together with all the old favourites including 'The Way Through the Woods' to make a thoroughly enchanting book. And perhaps most famous of all, included in this collection is Kipling's well-loved poem, 'If' – words that have spoken to the hearts of many a generation.

36600190R00063

Printed in Great Britain
by Amazon